A battle raged inside Melody.

Somewhere on that slide down the mountain she'd crossed a border into John North's territory. She'd come over to his side, and every internal sentry she'd set up to protect her hard-won peace was screaming for a halt.

His gaze raked her face a long, searching minute. He cupped the side of her face, pushed off her cap, letting her hair tumble loose.

Confused, enticed, comforted, she didn't know what to do anymore.

He laid his fingers over her lips. "Let me look at you."

Her heart slammed to a halt inside her chest. This madness had to stop now.

She pushed his hands aside and sat up. Moving away from his tempting hands, she snatched up her discarded hat.

"We need to get out of here." If her tone was harsh he was to blame—but, oh, how she longed to be back in his arms.

Dear Reader

I hope you enjoy THE SNOW-KISSED BRIDE. Thank you so much for picking it up in the first place. I was thrilled at the opportunity to write another book set in the magnificent Rocky Mountains. Though I do not live in the Rockies, I have spent many holidays there and can never get enough of their startling beauty.

Once, some years ago, my family and I camped above a crystal blue lake below a ragged mountain face. When we set up our tent the weather was warm and lovely. By morning the temperatures had dipped well below freezing. While we huddled in the van, drinking hot cocoa, striped chipmunks, oblivious to the cold, played around the camp.

Another time, an unexpected lightning storm surprised us with hailstones the size of baseballs. But, as with many mountain thunderstorms, the episode came and went in a matter of minutes, leaving only our dented van and a road filled with white ice as proof that it had even happened. As we discovered, and as John and Melody well know, unpredictability is part of the beauty, excitement and danger of the high Rockies.

I love hearing from readers. Please feel free to contact me through my website or blog at www.lindagoodnight.com

Until next time, happy reading, and may God bless.

Linda Goodnight

THE
SNOW-KISSED
BRIDE

BY
LINDA GOODNIGHT

MILLS & BOON®
Pure reading pleasure™

First published in Great Britain 2008
Harlequin Mills & Boon Limited,
Eton House, 18-24 Paradise Road, Richmond, Surrey TW9 1SR

© Linda Goodnight 2008

ISBN: 978 0 263 20394 3

Set in
07-11(

Printed and bound in Great Britain
by CPI Antony Rowe, Chippenham, Wiltshire

A romantic at heart, **Linda Goodnight** believes in the traditional values of family and home. Writing books enables her to share her certainty that, with faith and perseverance, love can last for ever and happy endings really are possible.

A native of Oklahoma, Linda lives in the country with her husband Gene, and Mugsy, an adorably obnoxious rat terrier. She and Gene have a blended family of six grown children. A former elementary schoolteacher, she is also a licenced nurse. When time permits, Linda loves to read, watch football and rodeo, and indulge in chocolate. She also enjoys taking long, calorie-burning walks in the nearby woods. Readers can write to her at linda@lindagoodnight.com

To the brave men and women
who train and work SAR dogs.

And also to the brilliant, loyal animals
who make a difference in so many lives.

Thank you for your dedication
and also for your invaluable contributions to this story.
Any mistakes are my own.

CHAPTER ONE

THE CALL FOR HELP came late at night. They usually did.

Only this one was the worst kind. A child. Lost in the unforgiving Colorado mountains.

Melody Crawford replaced the receiver and rolled out of the bed, shoving her feet into heavy boots as she pushed to stand. She'd been asleep less than thirty minutes.

Within another ten minutes, she was wide-awake, dressed for the frigid temperatures and rummaging in her "rescue closet" for the equipment she might need on the snow-covered trail. In more than fifteen years of rescue work, she'd never stopped feeling the adrenaline rush that came with a call.

Backpack always loaded and ready, she reached for her dog's leash and vest and heard the soft pad of canine footsteps crossing the kitchen and coming toward her in the narrow hallway.

It was Ace.

A little piece of her heart broke off.

Smile wide, thick fur fluffed and ready with one hard shake of his muscular form, the big, black-and-silver German shepherd gazed up at her in question. As always, Ace was ready to work, ready to run, ready to rescue the lost.

"Sorry, old chum," she said, laying one hand on the wide, intelligent head. "Not tonight."

Not any night in the near future, although Ace was the best air-scent search and rescue dog she'd ever trained.

As if he understood, the dog whined softly and collapsed at her feet to stare up at her with sad eyes.

"As soon as I get the money, boy. We'll have you fixed up and good as new."

But money, for Melody, was hard to come by. Even by training and boarding other people's dogs, her income was limited. The monthly check from her father's insurance barely covered necessities, and the surgery to correct Ace's damaged hind knees was expensive, far over her budget. But he'd sustained the injuries in the line of duty and deserved a chance to work again. Somehow, even if she had to take an outside job, she'd find a way to help her partner and friend.

The idea of working at a regular job made her shudder. Not that she was lazy. She worked long and hard up here in her secluded section of the mountains. It wasn't work that bothered her. It was people.

"Chili," she called softly and was not surprised to find the affable, reddish-brown Lab waiting quietly in the doorway behind her. Trained to search by air and ground, Chili was an excellent rescue dog who loved kids. With a little luck and by moving quickly, he had the best chance of finding the missing child.

With regrets to the depressed Ace, she snapped Chili into his bright orange rescue vest and, flashlight in hand, headed for her truck.

One step outside and she burrowed deeper into the muffler around her neck, thinking of the search to come.

The night was still as death and ten times as cold. Unless the lost kid was well dressed or found shelter, he was in serious trouble. The colder he became, the less scent he gave off. Without scent particles floating into Chili's incredible olfactory glands, the dog couldn't do his job.

The knowledge spurred Melody to work faster. If anyone could find the boy, she and Chili could do it. They were the best in the mountains. Maybe the best in the country. They never quit until the victim was found—alive or dead. She preferred alive.

As she passed the snug kennels, the rest of the dogs, all boarders in training, slipped out of their houses to stretch and shake beneath the white moon. Silver vapor puffed around their wide, sturdy heads. Like Ace, none of them would make the trip tonight. They weren't her dogs. They were brought to her by folks too busy or disinclined to do their own initial obedience training. Melody didn't mind. Working with dogs, anyone's dogs, was her life's work and ambition.

Ace and Chili, on the other hand, were her babies, her children, her family. She took care of them and they took care of her. Together, they didn't need anyone else, but a lot of people needed them. Occasionally. And when the need was met, people faded away from her wilderness cabin like the foggy vapor faded into the night.

People.

She touched the barely visible scar at her hairline.

Not her favorite species.

Intentionally, she turned her thoughts to the little boy lost somewhere beneath the flat white moon. He would be scared. Scared of the black, inky darkness. Scared of the night cries of wolf and owl. Scared even of the bare aspen limbs rubbing together like dead bones.

Kids were a different matter. She didn't consider them people yet. They didn't have prejudices and ulterior motives. They were at the mercy of adults, just as she'd been.

But no more. She was captain of her own fate, in control of her life, which did not include people most of the time. Thank God and Grandma Perkins, who'd left her this remote cabin more than sixteen years ago when life had been hell.

She opened the truck door and waited for Chili to leap easily into the passenger side, ready for the trip to a ranger station four miles down the mountain. As she climbed in behind her dog and cranked the engine, Melody wondered why she'd awakened tonight with the old memories so sharp.

But memories were okay, occasionally. They kept her focused, kept her mindful of why she'd never permanently leave this mountain again.

John North paced the command center he'd set up inside the ranger station near the small community of Glass Creek. Slowly, too slowly for his liking, the emergency personnel began to trickle in, waiting for their assignments. He tossed back the last dregs in his coffee cup, grimacing at the bitter taste.

As the new director of the equally new emergency management office in Dulcimer County, he had to do this first search right—and every search hereafter. Lives, as well as his livelihood, depended upon his exceptional training and expertise.

"How far away is that dog team?" he asked Brent Page, the county sheriff, who stood to one side chewing the end of a toothpick. John could see the man was aching for a cigarette but wouldn't give in while on duty.

"She'll be here."

He figured that. He'd called the woman, hadn't he? And

he distinctly remembered the soft, feminine sound of a voice still drenched in sleep.

As director, coordinating all the necessary team members was part of his job, right down to making the phone calls. As soon as all the emergency services were assembled, they could begin.

For the distraught parents, huddled with a female forest ranger at a small round table, the moment couldn't come too soon.

John laid out the topographical maps and mentally went through the scant information they had about the missing child.

Outside the station, truck motors roared and doors slammed. Voices carried on the still, thin air. A couple of park rangers came in followed by a slight woman with a happy-looking, red dog.

For John North time stopped. He stared at the woman. Bundled for the cold, she wore a bright yellow-and-blue ski suit and hooded parka. From within the frame of sheepskin she looked out over the assembled group, assessing, cautious, almost angry. She was both fearsome and fascinating, and John experienced a most unusual reaction. Interest. Attraction. He, who had sworn off women five years ago, was mesmerized.

The newcomer's face was delicate and pretty, though devoid of makeup. Her full lower lip looked soft and sensitive, kissable even, though he cursed himself for noticing at a time like this. But her eyes fascinated him the most. Pale, pale silver with edges of gold, her eyes were the strangest he'd ever seen. Not just the unusual, otherworldly color but something he saw in their depths, some deep and frightening knowledge. He'd seen that look before but he couldn't place where.

This must be the search and rescue team or "dog woman" as the other emergency personnel called her.

Shaking off the odd sensation that had gripped him the moment she walked into the station, John stepped forward. "I'm John North, director of operations."

He offered a hand. She didn't take it. If anything, she shrunk back, placing her palm on the dog at her side.

With those disturbing eyes, she quietly looked him over, and John was sure, found him woefully wanting.

"Melody Crawford," she said shortly. "This is Chili. Let's get started. Give me some details."

So much for introductions.

"The boy is ten. He and his father were hiking. Somehow they got separated."

"When?"

"About three hours ago." He pointed to the map spread out on a table next to the coffeepot, a telephone and a handheld radio. "Here."

He was acutely aware of the woman as she leaned forward and took note of the area. Her scent, as she leaned in, was a mix of cold air, warm woman and peppermint. She said nothing, only studied the map with the kind of intensity he'd witnessed during his many years as an Army Ranger.

Leaving her to the task, he began to disseminate duties to the various gathered personnel, all bearing maps and compasses and other search gear. The rangers and police officers would walk grids or drive the roads, hoping the boy would find his way out of the wilderness and onto a road. Others would ride snowmobiles or ATVs as far into the area as possible.

No other dog teams could be here anytime soon and time was too critical to wait. They'd have to go with this one woman and her Lab and pray that her reputation for success was warranted.

"We need to get started." He turned to Melody, who now waited quietly, while her canine made the rounds of the station, receiving pats and shaking hands. John found it especially interesting that the others present knew and liked her dog, but not one had spoken to the trainer. "You'll take the direct trail, following this grid."

"The map is inaccurate."

"What?"

"I'll follow the direct trail from where the boy was last seen, but this grid is off by at least a quarter of a mile."

"Great. Just great." Frustration burned in John's gut. Ever since taking this new position, he'd run into the same problem over and over again. All the data, the maps, the grids, the disaster plans were outdated. Coordinated out of the County Sheriff's office for years, emergency management was woefully lacking. That was why the mayor and governor had developed this new department in the first place, but as director, John had far more work to do than he'd imagined. And less time to do it. The governor had given him a year to prove the department was worth the extra funding.

"Do you know the area?"

Again that cool, cool stare from those bizarre eyes. "Of course. Does the family have any item that belonged to the boy? An item which hasn't been contaminated?"

"Is that necessary?" He'd always heard that SAR dogs could work without prescenting.

"No. But a scent helps get Chili moving much faster. And in case you haven't noticed, time is not on our side."

Though the comment bordered on sarcasm, she was right. The temperatures continued to fall. The boy was warmly dressed, which was a plus, but hypothermia remained a real threat.

"I'll ask the family." He made his way to the parents and returned with a stocking cap. He thrust it toward her. "Will this do?"

Strangely enough, she shrank back. "How many hands have touched it?"

"Mine, the dad's, and the boy's."

"It will have to do."

Without further ado, she spoke quietly to the dog, held the inside of the cap to his twitching black nose, and then left the command post.

Melody's insides trembled as she loaded Chili once more into the truck cab and climbed behind the wheel.

John North was military. She could see it in his precise bearing, hear it in the clipped, confident commands, *feel* it emanating from him in waves of danger. She knew his type. No pretty boy this. Rugged and masculine with snapping brown eyes and darker hair, John North was fit and powerful…

And military.

She laid her head on the steering wheel.

Upon hearing that the county had finally hired a full-time emergency management director, Melody had been pleased. The sheriff had done his best but was too understaffed to do an efficient job. Search and rescue had taken a backseat to all the duties of a sheriff to serve and protect, a fact of life that had severely hampered rescue operations. For a while, she'd worried they might hire Tad Clauson, a deputy who had lobbied long and hard for the development of an emergency management program within the county. While she agreed with his concept, she despised the deputy, who seemed intent on making her life miserable at every meeting.

But this man, this John North fellow, was far worse than Tad. He was military. He was deadly. And he scared her to pieces.

Chili, sensing her unease and wondering why they weren't moving whined softly and nudged at her hand as if to say, "Get moving, Mama, we have a kid to find."

With a shaky laugh, she cranked the engine. "Right. Focus, huh, boy? A lost kid is in a lot more trouble than we are."

Suddenly the passenger door was yanked open, and Melody changed her mind. John North slid onto the bench seat next to Chili.

Melody scowled, hoping to frighten him away. "What are you doing?"

"I thought I'd ride along with you, watch you work."

Her pulse ratcheted up to mach speed. "Chili and I work alone."

"Not this time. If I'm going to use your services, I need to see for myself that you know what you're doing."

In the darkness, lit only by the moon and the lights of vehicles beginning to move, he looked across at her, expression mild. There was a stubbornness about him, and a confidence that bordered on cockiness. He was the boss and she'd better get used to it.

She didn't like him.

"Suit yourself." She cranked the engine and drove in silence. The truck could only go so far before they'd have to hike into the wilderness to the area where the boy had last been seen. When they reached the vicinity, she parked the vehicle and got out, strapped on her backpack, leashed Chili and started through the woods without a word to her uninvited guest. If Mr. High and Mighty Military Man wanted to come, he'd better keep up.

He did. With little effort, he was beside her, his breath puffing gray smoke into the cold night.

Ignoring the man took effort, but Melody concentrated on her job with Chili. With soft commands, she unsnapped the dog, told him to search and waited while he gained his bearings. For several seconds, he stood, nose high, sorting the millions of scents that invaded his brain.

"What's he doing?"

"Processing information." She was accustomed to waiting quietly until Chili made his move. It was the way they worked. The dog searched for an inverted cone of scent. Once he tapped into it, he would be off, working in a zigzag as the cone of scent, hopefully, grew more and more narrow until they reached the missing person.

"How long does that take?"

She turned, shining the flashlight into his eyes. "I didn't ask you to come along."

John blinked and turned his head. At the same time, his right arm deflected the errant light. He tried to be gentle but the woman was getting under his skin. He'd come with her for the very reason he'd said, to observe her work. But if he was truthful, he wanted to observe more than that. Something about her unsettled him. As an Army Ranger, he'd spent many nights in the wilderness, most of them without sleep while waiting to complete a mission. Neither the rugged terrain nor the possibly long night ahead bothered him. Melody Crawford did.

"You aren't what I expected," he said.

She bristled, but didn't look at him. He was glad because

he'd had the stupid thought that her silvery-gold eyes might glow in the dark. "And why would you expect anything at all?"

"Well, you know." He shifted uncomfortably, wishing he'd kept his big mouth shut. Women didn't usually make him nervous. "I'd heard about you."

The air temperature around them seemed to drop ten degrees. "So they told you about the crazy woman who lives back in the mountains by herself with only dogs for company."

"Something like that."

By now, the dog must have caught the scent because he disappeared from their circle of light with a rustle of movement.

"Well, they're right. I am crazy. Keep that in mind while we're alone in these woods."

Dog leash rattling at her waist, she stalked away, heavy brown boots thudding the frozen earth.

John shrugged off her prickly attitude and followed. In thirteen years of military service, he'd dealt with his share of personalities. The mission was always the most important thing. In this case, his new mission was making sure his department did an exceptional job, every day, all the time. Anything less was unacceptable…and would cost him his new job and maybe even someone's life.

John North took the loss of lives personally, very personally.

Silent now, he fell into the familiar rhythm of moving through unfamiliar terrain with stealth and ease. Melody stayed directly ahead of him and, noticing the stiffness of her shoulders, John decided to keep the rest of his thoughts to himself.

He'd learned to ignore his body's needs, so the cold didn't bother him. He wondered, though, about Melody. She was tough and strong and warmly dressed, but she was a woman and not a very big one at that.

Yeah, and he was still a chauvinist who thought women needed to be cared for and protected. He shook his head ruefully. Hadn't his ex-wife taught him anything?

After about an hour in which he marveled at the woman's stamina, a series of short, happy yips rent the air. Melody stopped, spun around and said, "We found him." Her voice sounded as excited as the barks. "We did it."

John caught up to her and smiled. "Are you sure?"

She nodded curtly. "Chili's good."

"So are you. You trained him."

As if no one had ever noticed such a thing, she stopped dead still and her mouth dropped open. She blinked up at him, and John had the strongest urge to give her a hug. He didn't, of course. She'd likely punch him in the gut.

The dog barked again, more urgently now.

Melody's mouth snapped shut and she spun away. "Move it."

Hurrying over limbs and rocks and up a steep incline all slick with snow, they followed the sound.

"Does he ever get too far away for you to hear him bark?" John asked, huffing a bit to talk and keep up. The woman was in amazing physical condition.

"Sometimes. But he'll come back to me if that happens. I prefer he stay with the victim, especially on nights like this. He's a good source of heat."

"Makes sense."

The barking grew nearer and in less time than John could have hoped, the beam of his flashlight caught the gleaming eyes of the dog huddled next to a small boy. In seconds, they were beside the shivering child. While John checked him over, speaking in reassuring tones, Melody went to her knees and began rummaging in her backpack.

She looked up at him. "Start a fire. You know how, don't you?"

Was she intentionally trying to insult him? "In the pouring rain with two wet sticks."

The corner of her mouth twitched. She almost smiled. As he got busy proving his point, John couldn't help wondering what Melody Crawford would look like with a full-blown smile?

She baffled him, intrigued him and made him uncomfortable.

But she'd found the boy alive.

And he'd almost made her smile.

Next time, he would succeed.

CHAPTER TWO

THE NEXT MORNING word of the rescue had reached the newspaper and spread around the area. The phone rang off the hook with congratulations and reporters, some of whom decided to make the trek to Glass Falls for up close and personal interviews with John and the other rescuers.

John fought off a grimace as yet another reporter snapped a photo of him. His small office was full of newspeople, along with city officials eager to have their name and photo in the papers and on television.

"What can you tell us about the boy, Mr. North?"

He'd told the story so many times, he was getting annoyed, but for the sake of his new department, positive publicity was a good thing. "He was taken by ambulance to a Boulder hospital. You'll have to talk to them for complete information, but about fifteen minutes ago, I received word that he was asking for pizza and would recover fully."

The boy also suffered some hypothermia and mild frostbite to the fingers, but that was the family's story to tell, not John's.

"Who found him?"

"A volunteer search and rescue dog and his trainer, Melody Crawford. They were pretty amazing to watch." In fact, for all her prickly attitude with him, she and her dog were poetry in motion. While he had built a fire and radioed the news to other rescuers, she wrapped the boy in a blanket from her backpack and prepared a cup of hot bouillon. All the while, she was gentle and reassuring to the frightened ten-year-old, far different from the way she treated adults.

Yes, Melody Crawford was an interesting woman.

"Is Miss Crawford available for an interview?" another reporter asked.

Somehow John was sure she would not be. "Not to my knowledge."

In all the fuss and bother of last night's reunion with parents and preparation to transport the boy to the hospital, Melody and Chili had simply disappeared without a word. Once back in the command center, John had looked around to thank her and offer a cup of coffee and a sandwich only to find she was gone. He'd even looked outside and sure enough, her gray truck no longer occupied the parking space.

A man had to admire a woman like that. She wasn't in it for the glory; that was for sure. Once the mission was accomplished, she quietly disappeared.

As an ex-Ranger, he could relate.

After another thirty minutes of questions and answers, the newspeople disappeared and with them the city officials. John closed the door on the last one with a sigh of relief. He was accustomed to working with a unit and in mixed chaos, but a few minutes of peace and quiet after a sleepless night was more than welcome right now.

But before he could sit down at his desk, the telephone rang again. He rubbed a hand over the back of his neck and gave a short laugh. Being a one-man office at the moment, he answered the call himself. On the other end was the governor, offering enthusiastic congratulations.

Good. If the governor was happy, the chances for the program to move forward increased exponentially.

"Yes, sir," he said. "Thank you, sir. The credit goes to Miss Crawford and her dog. They found the boy."

Even a year postdischarge, military commands and protocol echoed in John's head, too ingrained to go away. He even said "yes, sir" and "no, sir" to telemarketers.

As he hung up the phone, Deputy Sheriff Tad Clauson sauntered into his office and scraped a chair close to John's desk. Sunlight streaming in from the window glinted on the man's perfectly groomed blond hair. A pair of aviator sunglasses peeked from his uniform pocket. Clauson was the type to play the part of slick cop to the hilt.

"You're becoming quite the celebrity, aren't you, North?"

What was this all about? John pushed back in his chair and assessed the situation, waiting two beats before answering. "Small towns like big news."

"Guess that's why you tagged along with the dog woman." Tad's face, while smiling, didn't look all that friendly. If the man had something to say he needed to spit it out.

John put his elbows on the desk and steepled his fingers. This wasn't the first time Tad had come around, dropping snide remarks. "I'm not sure I follow."

"Sure you do. The dog was the likely candidate to find the boy, which put you right in the middle of glory land." Before John had time to think up a reply that didn't include curse words, Tad said, "Or was it the dog woman you were interested in? Spooky-looking if you ask me, with those weird witch's eyes, but some men go for that kind of thing."

In John's line of work jerks abounded. He didn't let the deputy ruffle his composure, although the insult to both him and Melody were clear. "Are you intentionally trying to annoy me, Tad?"

"Just kidding, man, just kidding." The deputy bounced up from his chair with a laugh then clapped his hand onto John's desk. "I came by to invite you over tonight. Marla's in the mood for company and cooking up her special enchilada casserole. Sheriff and his wife and a few others will be there. What do you say?"

John gave the invitation some thought. He and Tad went way back to high school days, but Tad had changed. Well, so had he, come to think of it. Time and experience did that to a man.

He wasn't sure if he liked Tad Clauson anymore, but he wasn't one to make snap judgments about people. Situations, yes. People, no, though his instincts seldom failed him.

"Thanks, I appreciate the offer." Getting reacquainted with the town he'd left years ago was an important part of his work. The more he knew, the better prepared he could be in an emergency situation.

Tad slapped his shoulder and pointed at him, fingers cocked like a pistol. "Seven sharp or Marla will set the dogs on you."

With another laugh, the man left. John stared after him in deep thought. He had a feeling the visit was more than an invitation to dinner, though he had no idea why.

The roller chair rattled as he pushed away from his desk and crossed the hall to the sheriff's office. The county courthouse housed all the city officials, making contact easy and efficient. It was about the only efficient thing he'd found so far.

Sheriff Brent Page waved him inside as he ended a telephone conversation. In his midfifties, the sheriff remained in decent shape, though he sported a slight paunch.

"Come in here, North." He removed a cigarette from a package and stuck it in his mouth unlit.

"Those will kill you."

"Man's gotta die of something."

John grunted. He could think of other more pleasant and definitely quicker methods. "What's going on with Tad Clauson?"

"Getting under your skin?"

"Some. We were friends in high school so I'm not sure what the deal is. He seems to resent me for some reason."

"That's a fact."

"Why?"

Brent tongued the cigarette from one side of his mouth to the other. Smoking was outlawed in the courthouse, so all he could do was fondle the cancer stick.

"Figured you knew. Tad wanted your job. When the city officials first came up with the notion, spurred on by our total incompetence in the spring floods a couple of years ago, Tad put in his application."

"Why did they turn him down?"

"Now, that I don't know. I could guess, and so can you if you pay attention. Governor also seemed more interested in a man of your experience, a military man. Veteran's preference and all that. Tad's a good deputy, not a bad sort. We gave him a bump in pay, sort of a Band-Aid to his wounded ego. That's the problem. Pride. Don't take it personally. Just do the job the state is paying you to do."

But John heard what the sheriff wasn't saying about the deputy. Watch your back and don't screw up. "I guess I have a lot to prove to everyone, not just Tad."

"Yes, you do, and not long to prove it."

"Which is actually the reason I wanted to talk to you." He

tossed a sheaf of papers on the sheriff's desk. "I have ideas to improve the system, starting with a new grid around all the campgrounds and trailheads. Everything I've got to work with is at least ten years old."

Newer computerized satellite maps were helpful but not precise enough for search and rescue.

"Some a lot older."

"Exactly. To do that, I need manpower."

"Don't have it. You'll have to recruit your own."

"That's where I want your advice. I need a list of people who know these mountains and trails. People who have the time and willingness to spend days and weeks, maybe months, in the wilderness without much in the way of compensation."

He was setting out a monumental task, and both he and Brent knew it.

Brent took the cigarette from his mouth and held the tips with both index fingers and thumbs. He studied the filter as though the names were engraved thereon.

"Couple of people come to mind. Clovis Holland, for one, but he's getting up in years. Might not have the stamina."

"Who else?"

Brent poked the cigarette into his shirt pocket, gave it a loving pat and said, "Melody Crawford."

Fists on his hips, John shook his head. "I don't think she likes me much."

"Melody Crawford doesn't like anybody that I know of unless they have four legs and a tail, but no one knows these mountains better. She spends days on end tracking and working with her dogs, exploring the trails and off-grid areas anyway. Since she volunteers for search and rescue, she might be willing. She's for sure your best bet and she's danged good at her job."

"Can't argue that." Last night, she and Chili had been like one mind with two bodies.

"A handsome young rogue such as yourself can surely find a way to convince Mel to give you a hand."

John answered with a grunt. "Don't bet on it."

"Well, give Clovis a call and then talk to Melody. Doesn't cost anything to ask."

"Will do. Thank you, sir." With a one-finger salute, John did an about-face and returned to his office. The sheriff had given him some food for thought.

Rummaging in the stack of papers on his desk, he took a notepad and made his usual list for the day. The duty of creating an entirely new department single-handedly was daunting, but he was up for the task. Of particular importance was public awareness. He was setting up speaking engagements with the county schools and civic groups, arranging meetings with all hospitals, municipal facilities, schools, etc. to develop new, workable disaster plans. He was still making the rounds of all the towns, getting personally acquainted with emergency personnel that he might have to call upon.

Then there was the ongoing worry of gathering accurate data, resources, maps and other tools to make rescue operations function smoothly. As of today, that was priority one.

He shuddered to think what might have happened last night if Melody had not known the grid map was inaccurate.

Resolutely, he found Clovis's phone number, only to hear that the man was in the hospital having a hip replaced.

"One down and one to go," he muttered as he rustled papers looking for Melody Crawford's phone number. Creating a Rolodex or computer file of phone numbers was another thing he needed to do.

Finding the number, he started to dial and then changed his mind. A job offer to a prickly woman should be presented in person.

He tossed his pencil on the desk, got up and grabbed his coat from the rack by the door.

She was probably going to turn him down, but she would have to do it to his face.

Melody cradled the telephone against her ear and gnawed on the side of her thumbnail while the veterinarian in Boulder told her what to do for Ace's aching knees. The German shepherd was so stiff this morning, Melody had cried to see him trying to walk to his feed.

"Surgery is the only real solution, Miss Crawford," the doctor said.

"I know. I'm working on it."

"If it's helpful, we take credit cards."

That had to be repaid. "I'll get back to you. Thanks, Dr. Lampert."

After ringing off, Melody heated cloths in the microwave and wrapped them around Ace's hind legs. The big dog lay quietly on his fluffy rug next to the heater, trusting her to do the right thing. His sweet, accepting attitude made her feel all the worse. She wanted to do the right thing. She just didn't have the money. The credit card offer lingered in her mind. If she could find a way to make those payments…

Once Ace was situated and as comfortable as she could make him, she slipped on her coat to take care of the kennel dogs. Chili stood and stretched, eager to go out with her.

"Not this time, Chili. You need to rest." She'd fed him his favorite treat, a hamburger patty, last night when they'd arrived home. Both of them were exhausted, but the adrenaline rush of success took time to wear off.

"You were magnificent, boy," she said, stroking the soft red fur. He looked up at her with all the confidence and joy any dog could have. He was good. He knew it and was very proud of that fact. A child was safely reunited with his parents because of Chili's efforts. As his trainer, nothing was more fulfilling for Melody.

Leaving her dogs inside, she stepped out into the crisp morning. The sun was out, startling in its brightness. Overhead a red-tailed hawk circled, looking for breakfast while a downy woodpecker rat-a-tat-tatted at the limb of an aspen. The earth smelled fresh and expectant. A new snow had fallen during the night and she was thankful again they'd found the boy before the weather moved through.

Spring was around the corner, if you could call it that. At this altitude, there were really only two seasons, June and winter. Spring was glorious when the tiny alpine flowers sprinkled the countryside. But with the spring, came the thaws and dangers of flooding along with unpredictable thunder and snowstorms, and the tourists began to trickle in, camping, hiking, exploring her beloved back country. Her search and rescue work always accelerated in spring when unsuspecting tourists were trapped in a sudden snowstorm or lost at night in light clothing when the temperatures plummeted.

She opened the kennel and went in, greeted by six excited dogs of various breeds. Each day, she worked with each of them according to his or her level, teaching obedience or taking them a step further to tracking and trailing. First, they got to run and play for the pure joy of life.

After hugging each one around the neck and offering soft

words of praise, she opened the gate wide and let them out. They bounded forth, running in circles and barking, powdery snow spraying up around them.

Melody absorbed their pleasure and laughed, spinning slowly in a circle, arms wide to her sides. This was her refuge and she loved being here alone on top of the world with all of nature spread out before her.

Her little cabin sat in a small clearing at the end of a two-mile driveway that was really more of a trail. Only a four-wheel-drive vehicle or ATV could manage the rugged climb. Around the cabin were miles and miles of wilderness. Aspens and pines as far as the eye could see sheltered dozens of wild species, and Melody had seen most of them at one time or another. Even grizzlies or mountain cats occasionally wandered too close for comfort and she'd learned to watch for them. Fortunately, the dogs would smell the predators and signal a warning long before the animals made their presence known to her.

An Australian shepherd, still learning his manners, leaped at her from behind and knocked her to the ground. She corrected him, watching his intelligent face take in the message that this was not a good thing. And then, she rubbed the thick fur around his neck and laughed. As if the action was a signal, the other five dogs bounded up, eager to play.

In the next moment, she was on the ground wrestling and rolling in the snow with six, excited dogs. Laughter bubbled up and spilled over, echoing out across the pristine snow.

There was nothing like a warm, wiggling, furry dog to make her forget.

Suddenly, the air changed and a voice broke through her laughter.

A male voice.

"Looks like you're having fun."

The sharp surge of adrenaline fear burned her nerve endings. Melody thrashed against the bundles of fur and leaped to her feet. Her heart thundered in her ears like a wild, spring storm.

She spun toward the intruder. Tall, dark, military.

"Miss Crawford? Remember me? John North." She must have looked terrified because he held both hands out to his sides as if to indicate he carried no weapon.

Melody didn't care if he had a weapon or not. He was dangerous. She swallowed the thick taste of fear. No use letting him see how much his presence disturbed her. "What are you doing here?"

"I've come to talk to you about something."

"I'm not interested." She turned to catch the Australian shepherd by the collar and leashed him. Calling each of the dogs by name, she headed toward the kennels.

John North fell in step beside her. "How would you know without hearing me out?"

Why couldn't the man go away? He was big and threatening and too friendly. Last night, he'd also been helpful. She didn't want to appreciate that. She only wanted him to go away.

"I just know." She signaled the dogs into the kennel and headed toward their feed barrel. "How did you find me?"

Grinning, he took the filled bucket from her. "I have maps."

"Inaccurate ones." She huffed and reached for the bucket. "Let me have that. I can take care of these animals myself."

"I have no doubt of that." But he didn't return the bucket. Instead he shook the kibble into the dishes, patting canine heads as he went. He liked dogs. That much was in his favor.

Melody went inside the heated area of the kennel for fresh water. "So what do you want?"

"I need a favor."

"No."

He laughed. She liked the sound. She also liked the little laugh crinkles around his mouth.

"You're a hard case," he said.

"And don't forget it."

She completed the task of feeding and watering the dogs. All the while, John North remained by her side, helping without being asked, and generally making her uncomfortable.

"The inaccurate maps are why I'm here."

She ignored him.

He stood against one corner of the chain-link fence talking anyway. "One of my goals as director of emergency management is to create a more effective, streamlined system. When lives are at stake, we need to move fast and be confident that our equipment won't let us down."

"Here." She thrust a shovel at him. "If you want to be of help, you can shovel manure."

The crinkles reappeared around his mouth. He took the shovel and got to work. "I've done worse. You're not going to run me off until you hear me out."

"Maybe you're the hard case."

"And don't you forget it," he said, echoing her words. "I need your help. You know these woods and mountains better than just about anyone around. I want to remap and regrid a five-mile radius around all the main areas of entrance into the wilderness."

"Big job." But a good idea. She'd stopped looking at the maps from the sheriff's office, relying instead on her memory.

They were that outdated. If John North could accomplish such a task, more power to him. "Why are you telling me?"

"Because I need your help. We can do it."

Melody's gaze flew up to meet his. "We?"

Was he asking what she thought he was asking?

Snapping brown eyes, too smart for their own good, stared back. "You and me. By foot or snowmobile, whatever it takes. We'll reconcile the old maps and newer satellite images with hands-on reality." He propped the shovel against the fence and crossed his arms. "What do you think?"

Melody seldom noticed the cold but suddenly she was chilled to the bone. Spend months traipsing the wilderness with John North, a man with military oozing out of him? A man who had been trained to kill?

Not a snowball's chance, buddy. That's what she thought.

She stored the shovel and bucket and led the way out of the kennel. The dogs looked at her, bewildered. She'd come back later for their training session, once she was rid of John North.

"I'm sorry, Mr. North. You'll have to find someone else. I'm not interested."

And before he could say another word and make her feel guilty, she stalked into the house and locked the door.

CHAPTER THREE

WATER ROARED over Glass Falls and tumbled into the swollen creek below. The spring thaws had begun.

John made a note of his location on a handheld computer, jotting down the coordinates and details, then hitched his small knapsack and started back to the main trail. At this rate, the mapping project would be done right before his retirement party in twenty years. Maybe.

As he picked his way over the fallen limbs and thick, melting snow, he absorbed the sights and smells of the woods. Wet and fertile, woodsy with the first hint of green. This was the type of environment in which he thrived. After all those years serving in every known climate and terrain as a Ranger, the outdoors was in his blood. He loved being out here in the rain or cold or heat or whatever.

Maybe that's why Melody Crawford intrigued him so much. He could relate to her solitude. He liked being alone in the wilderness, but he also liked to be with people on occasion. That's where he and the woman with the fascinating eyes differed. She'd walked away and left him standing in her yard as though he didn't exist.

A man couldn't help taking that a tad personally.

He knew he'd startled her, walking up on her that way. But when he'd arrived at her cabin after the long, bumpy drive, he'd heard her laughter coming from behind the house. Sounds carry forever in the thin mountain air and her laugh was so beautiful and free, he'd had to know what caused it. As he'd rounded the corner of the house, he'd seen her there, rolling in the snow with a half-dozen big dogs, laughing for all she was worth.

For a moment, he'd stood there in the sunshine listening and watching, an odd sensation swelling in his chest. She was really lovely when she laughed.

Then, when she'd bolted upright, startled by his sudden appearance, he'd lost his breath.

The previous night, she'd been bundled from head to toe. That morning the dogs had wrestled away her stocking cap and her hair fell around her face in disarray. She had interesting hair, black as midnight and chopped in some jagged, shaggy hairdo as if she cut it herself or frequented the best Beverly Hills salon. He suspected the former was the case. Her ebony locks were the perfect vehicle for those strange silvery-gold eyes. No wonder Tad had called her a black cat.

There was something about her, all right. He couldn't get her out of his head. If only she would agree to help out with the mapping project, he could spend enough time with her to figure out why she fascinated him so much.

But she'd turned him down flat. So had everyone else. He'd called and visited every possible candidate for the project. Mostly, they'd laughed him off.

By now, he'd reached his truck. A striped chipmunk sat on the hood nibbling his lunch. At John's approach, the cute critter scampered up a tree, chattering and scolding.

John tossed his knapsack into the seat and climbed inside. He was speaking to a civic group this afternoon, the Kiwanis Club. Friday, he'd drive down to Denver for a meeting with the governor. He wished he had more progress to report, although he felt pretty good about all that had been done in a short time.

In fact, he felt so good about the progress he'd ordered tickets to a Denver Nuggets' basketball game for him and a couple of friends. Nothing like an arena full of screaming fans, flashy cheerleaders and a couple of bratwursts to recharge a man's engine.

On the way back to the courthouse, he stopped for lunch at one of the cafés on Main Street. The county seat of Glass Falls was a small town, but outlying towns were even smaller. Such was the way of mountain regions. They boomed during tourist season, but only the rugged stayed year-round. Tourist season was about to begin in earnest and with the increase in people the potential for disasters rose. He wanted to be ready.

The café's occupants greeted him by name and he stopped to talk to first one and then another. When he'd finally ordered his hamburger, Tad Clauson came through the door. Dressed in uniform, the man took a few admiring stares from the local ladies. He knew it, too.

"North," he said. "Mind if I join you?"

"Pull up a chair." John pushed the menu toward the other man. "How's it going?"

"Okay. Wanted to tell you about a bear sighting up on the ridge above Foster's Pass. A grizzly tore up a couple of sheep."

Bear sightings belonged to the forestry service, not to his department. "Guess he woke up from his winter nap hungry and in a bad mood."

"Got that right. So how's the program coming along? Marla heard you had an appointment with the governor."

John figured there was more to this visit than a bear sighting. "Friday. I think he'll be pleased."

"Any luck with that special project of yours?"

Everyone in the county knew he was determined to remap the danger areas. "Some. I'm still looking for volunteer help."

The waitress brought his burger and took Tad's order. "You'll have to pay for that kind of work."

"Can't. No money in the budget. You wouldn't want to spend your free time roaming the mountain wilderness, would you?"

"I thought that spooky dog woman was going to help you?"

John opened the top of his burger to sprinkle on salt and pepper. "Turned me down."

"Told you she was weird."

"You turned me down, too. Does that make you weird?" John bit into his burger. The spurt of rich beef flavor and spicy mustard was just what he was after.

"Ha. Good one. I have a job. She doesn't. She has time. All she does is train those dogs and traipse the wilderness anyway. She's always out there. I don't know why she won't make herself useful."

"How do you know so much about her activities?"

Tad shifted uncomfortably. "Never said I did. Just a guess."

John wondered.

The waitress brought Tad's burger and fries. Steam and a heavenly aroma wafted over the table as the deputy dipped a fry into ketchup.

"Money talks," Tad went on. "You're the governor's pal. Can't you squeeze a little more money out of him?"

"I've already tried."

Tad laughed. "Guess the governor doesn't love you as much as you thought."

John took another bite of his juicy burger and chewed, thinking about more important things than Clauson's jealousy. Money did talk and a woman living alone with no outside job could probably use a little extra. The trouble was, his department's budget had very little wiggle room.

Suddenly, a thought hit him. His pay was more than adequate and his needs simple. Why not pay her out of his pocket? Funds might be tight for a while, but he could manage. On the heels of that thought came another. Melody Crawford didn't like him, or at least seemed not to. She might be insulted or suspicious if the offer of pay appeared to come from his account.

Fair enough. A Ranger did what he had to do in order to accomplish a mission. He'd present the offer as temporary employment with the Department of Emergency Management. She never needed to know the money came from him.

With an inner smile, John took a burning sip of cola, satisfied that he'd arrived at a workable solution. That is, if Melody Crawford would cooperate.

As the sheriff said, it never hurt to ask. He needed Melody's knowledge of the mountains. He also needed something else from her, though he hadn't quite figured out what that was. But he would.

Melody walked the Australian shepherd, Kip, around the wooden slide letting him explore the new obstacle before taking him up. The slide was one of several pieces of training equipment she'd built behind the kennels. After a minute, she guided the dog onto the slide and urged him upward, using his squeaky toy as a lure. Crouched down and nervous, he crept along at a snail's pace.

When he reached the top of the slide, she gave him the toy and lifted him down. He was trembling. Not good. Because of his timidity, she was about to come to the conclusion that Kip would not make a good SAR dog. He would, however, be a wonderful and obedient pet to his family.

"Sit. Stay," she commanded, using a kind but firm voice while holding her palm down and out in a hand signal. When the dog obeyed promptly, Melody rewarded him with lavish praise. Her trainees started on treats and were gradually weaned to enjoy only praise or a play toy. Kip loved praise best of all.

She walked a short distance away, clapped her hands loudly and made a variety of noises. The other dogs began to bark. Still Kip held his position, expression eager to please.

"Good boy. Good Kip." She counted to ten and called, "Kip. Come."

He bounded toward her and she rewarded him, ruffling his shaggy head with her hands. "Good boy, good Kip. Time to go in."

The shepherd pranced along beside her and went readily into his pen. The remaining two dogs were eager for their turn but the sun was already high in the sky and her belly rumbled. "Later, guys. After my lunch."

Feeling successful and positive, she hummed a tune as she let herself in through the back door of the cabin. The warm smell of vegetable stew, simmering in the Crock-Pot, circled around her head. The scent was so strong and wonderful, Melody made a moaning noise. She laughingly thought this must be the way her dogs felt when they scented a search victim.

Hanging her jacket on the peg by the door, she went through the kitchen and toward the bathroom to wash up.

A soft whine stopped her in the hallway. "Chili? Ace?"

Chili came around the door from the bedroom, his eyes worried, body tense.

"What's wrong, buddy?"

Body language urgent, the lab "told" her something was amiss. Then he turned and hurried back into the bedroom. The whine came again. Ace's whine. *Oh, no.* With trepidation in her heart, Melody followed the sound.

Ace lay on the floor beside her bed, distress emanating from his noble form. "Ace? What's the matter, old chum?"

Melody went down on her knees beside the dog. Chili sidled up close to her. She pushed him away. Something was wrong with the shepherd. He'd been asleep earlier when she'd gone out to train, but now he struggled to stand, clearly in pain. He made it halfway up before collapsing with a yip.

Tears burned at the back of Melody's eyes. Her best friend's knees had finally frozen into position. He could no longer stand without terrible pain. The vet had warned her this might happen if the surgery didn't take place soon.

She'd failed him. The tears came in earnest now as she buried her face against his fur.

"I'm sorry, baby, I'm sorry. We'll go to the vet today." No matter the cost, Ace was going to have that surgery. She'd take out a loan and find a job waiting tables or whatever was available. She'd been selfish too long and look what had happened.

Gently, she lifted her canine friend and carried him into the warmer living room and placed him on the rug. When he was comfortable, she gave him one of the pills the vet had pre-scribed, and then put his hot packs in the microwave.

She was watching the turntable spin round and round, tears blurring her vision, when someone banged on the front door. She jerked, startled as always. Visitors were a rare occurrence.

Ace immediately alerted, barking for all he was worth. The protective sound brought more tears. The sweet dog would try to protect her no matter how badly he hurt. Reassuring the dog that she was safe, she dashed at the tears and went to the door.

John North stood on her small wooden step. Maybe she wasn't safe after all.

Before she had a chance to ask him what he wanted now, he spoke. "What's wrong? Why are you crying?"

She shook her head, not wanting to cry in his presence but unable to staunch the tears.

"Are you all right?" When she didn't answer, he pushed past her into the living and looked around. His stance was fierce and warrior-like, ready for battle. A shiver ran down her spine.

"I'm fine. Please" was all she could get out. She wanted him to leave.

Instead, he took her shoulders and walked her to a chair. "Can I do anything?"

She pushed right back out of the chair and went to Ace. Every hair on the shepherd's back stood up. "My dog is sick. I've got it under control."

John North was smart enough to keep his distance from the distressed animal. The man stood, tall and straight, next to the chair she'd vacated. "What's wrong with him?"

Melody explained the knee injury and the need for surgery, leaving out the budget problem.

"When is he scheduled?"

"I'm working on it." She pushed to her feet. "Right now, he needs the hot packs I have in the microwave."

"Can I help?"

Only if you have a few thousand extra dollars on you. "No."

"Will he let me pet him?"

"He will now." She stroked Ace's face and crooned, "He's a friend, boy. It's okay."

True or not, she didn't want to upset the suffering dog.

Then she went into the kitchen for the warm packs.

When she returned, Ace appeared to have found a friend for life. His big head rested in the man's lap and he looked more relaxed than she'd seen him in days. "What did you do to him?"

John North's mouth quirked. "An old military secret. If I tell you, I'll have to kill you."

The silly phrase made her insides tremble. She knew not to react to the words. People said them all the time. They just didn't realize what they were saying.

Her shaky hand went to her forehead, touching the place where the bullet had penetrated. The scar was practically invisible to others, but not to her. Never to her.

She had to get a grip. Ace was the one in need here, not her. She could take care of herself.

To cover her nerves, she asked, "Would you like some coffee?"

John North's wide capable fingers gently stroked Ace's muzzle. The shepherd emitted a sigh of deep relaxation. "Is that what smells so incredible?"

"That's stew."

He jacked an eyebrow and made a soft *mmm* sound. Melody was tempted to laugh. "Are you hinting?"

"A single guy gets hungry for home cooking."

"You're a troublesome man, John North." But her dogs liked him.

"I came to make you an offer."

"For my stew? Six dollars a bowl."

Those crinkles appeared in the sides of his face. She liked those crinkles. She didn't like him. She couldn't.

"To work for me on the mapping project."

"Sorry, I already said no."

"What if I were to pay you?"

Her head jerked upward. "I thought it was a voluntary position."

"I need someone with your knowledge, so I juggled the budget. You're worth the money." He named a nice hourly wage.

She blinked, stunned and excited at the same time. "This is a joke, right? Tad Clauson sent you up here to torment me."

"Tad?" He frowned. "I run my own department, Melody. And that department needs you. So what do you say? Will you help me, and in the process save lives?"

The offer ping-ponged around in her head, enticing. Could she do it? Could she spend day after day alone in the wilderness with a man who reminded her of an unspeakable past?

Ace tried to shift positions to snuggle closer to the big military man. The pain was too much. The whine became a groan.

That was all the convincing Melody required.

No matter how much the man disturbed her, she'd promised Ace that surgery.

So for the next few months, she would work for John North and earn that money.

Even if it killed her.

She only hoped she didn't lose what was left of her mind.

CHAPTER FOUR

TROUBLE BEGAN on the very first day out.

The roar of a loud motor was Melody's first clue that this was going to be every bit as difficult as she'd expected.

John North, dressed in all black and looking as big and dangerous and scary as one of Hells Angels, rode up on an ATV. One, single ATV.

Melody eyed the machine with trepidation. John North expected her to ride on that. With him. At the thought, her nerve endings jittered like frayed electric wires. She worried she might short out, blow a fuse.

"I prefer to hike."

He jabbed a thumb over his shoulder.

"We ride," he said simply as though his order was not to be questioned.

"The dogs—" she started.

"They run." He patted the seat behind him.

Melody sucked in a breath of chilled morning air and considered calling the whole thing off. But the fantasy lasted only a second. Ace was in the hospital, his surgery scheduled today. It was too late to back out now.

The air was crisp and clean and still and the sun bright, but

Melody knew better than to trust the weather any more than she trusted John North. A lightning storm or wind or whiteout could come at any time. Such was the excitement and trepidation of the Rockies.

Be aware or die. Melody had lived by that motto most of her life.

She tossed her backpack onto the rear rack of the machine, attaching it with Velcro as North had done. Then, ignoring his tilted grin and the dread in the pit of her stomach, she swung one leg over to straddle the seat behind him.

He gunned the machine and laughed when she jumped. She thumped his shoulder with the flat of her hand, felt the hard muscle flex, heard the whisper of skin against waterproof nylon. Her instant reaction was withdrawal. Don't touch him. Don't let him touch her.

John North was of another mindset.

"Grab on," he said with a little too much glee and kicked the machine into gear.

Melody grabbed the sides of the seat, desperately trying to keep a space between her body and his. She couldn't risk the contact, the intimacy, the vulnerability. After a few miles of jouncing and struggling, the task proved exhausting. Her neck and shoulders screamed for relief.

Following one particular rocky jarring on a steep climb, North said, "Hold on to me. I won't bite."

Right. And she was Little Red Riding Hood.

But hiking required all the strength and energy she could conserve, so stealing herself for the unwanted contact, Melody gripped the sides of North's jacket. One solid bump and her fingers slipped. Impatiently, North grabbed her fisted hand and placed it securely around his waist. Her fingers landed just over his belly button.

"Hold *on*," he said, less patient now.

Melody clinched her eyes and put both arms around him, locking her fingers together. Stiffly, she tried to maintain that infinitesimal space between her chest and his back. Her shoulders ached from the effort until, defeated, she leaned in.

Every alarm bell screamed red alert. His back muscles were hard and fit and masculine. They flexed and shifted with the machine and the terrain, a source of repressed power that had her shivering, though whether in fear or admiration, she couldn't say.

Being a dog woman who lived her life according to the scent of her trainees, her own sense of smell was amplified. And John North smelled earthy, vibrant, *hot.* Even in the cold, his skin radiated heat. The dogs would have an easy time of tracking John North. So would she.

As the ATV started down an incline, Melody was thrust forward, closer, her breasts touching his back so that she was more aware of them than she had been in a long time. She hoped North didn't notice.

A rocky, crystal creek loomed. Water splashed as the ATV traversed the narrow span. Melody relented and rested her cheek against John's back. That's when she realized he'd placed one of his hands over hers, trapping her fingers against his belly. Even in heavy gloves, his strength was evident.

Melody swallowed a lump of anxiety. Alone in the wilderness with John North. What had she been thinking?

By the third day, Melody was still waiting for the ax to fall.

So far, North had been the gentleman, bossy but professional, lulling her into believing he might be one of the good guys.

But Melody had stopped believing in good guys a long time ago.

On that first day, they'd ridden the ATV as far as possible and hiked the rest of the way, donning snowshoes whenever necessary. This had become their modus operandi. Today was no different. She'd almost become accustomed to having her body pressed close to his on the four-wheeler. To having her senses run amok and torment her. To noticing him too much.

Almost.

If she thought about John North more than was prudent, she considered the action self-preservation, not attraction. She wouldn't fall into that trap.

Boots crunched on snow as she traipsed behind the man in question through dark forests and across rocky overhangs. Snow drooped on evergreens, stunning in beauty, shifting and filtering to the ground in silent submission as the invading humans jostled past.

As she had every day, Melody was careful to keep John North in her sights at all times. As long as she could see him, she could protect herself. The task was more exhausting than the work they were doing.

Eyes gritty, she yawned. The last couple of nights, she'd slept little. She blamed John North for that.

In his quiet, authoritative way he'd invaded her solitude. Melody resented him for that, too. Though she'd allowed the invasion for her own reasons, she would make very certain he did not also penetrate her carefully erected fortress. She would watch him. Oh, yes, she was on guard.

Chili and Casey, a cheerful border collie and one of her trainees, cavorted along next to her, more for companionship than assistance. Their jobs were search and rescue, not trailhead grids, but with them along Melody didn't have to interact as much with the unnerving military man.

He'd never said he was military and she hadn't asked, but she knew.

No one lived through hell without recognizing the devil.

Normally when hiking, she sang at the top of her voice to warn wildlife, particularly bear and moose of her presence. Now she clacked her trekking poles together and remained otherwise silent. The animal she feared the most was human. Let him ward off the other predators.

Her gloved hands fidgeted on the tiny handheld computer John North had given her. She knew little of computers, considering she couldn't afford one, but she wasn't stupid, either. An electronic copy of hand-drawn and written notes would prove useful, fast to access and highly portable, as well as offering the ability to share quickly and easily with other team members. Coupled with the latest blurry satellite maps in her knapsack and her years of wilderness trekking, the newly collected data would help save lives.

Since beginning this seemingly impossible task, she and her partner had logged dozens of changes—recently opened trails, crevices, rock slides, washed-out pathways, shifted or newly formed creek beds, animal sightings. They'd closed one trail and put up warning signs. The trail had washed out and simply wasn't there any longer. The only constant here in the mountain wilderness was change. Weather change, geographical change.

Pushing her sunglasses up and over her cap, she paused to enter data into the computer.

John North whirled in the trail, aware she'd stopped, though she hadn't made a sound. That was one of the many things about him that kept her nerves on edge. He had uncanny senses, better even than hers, though she wouldn't tell him so.

"Might as well make camp. Have lunch," he said, returning to where she stood. For a military guy, he looked especially scruffy today. At some point, he'd discarded his outer jacket and now wore a black-and-gray hoodie, the hood shoved back so that his dark hair was tousled. But the camo pants and boots were what gave her pause. Melody hated camo.

She shifted back a step, pulse skittering. John North had a habit of coming too close for comfort.

Even with that extra space between them, Melody winded him, as the dogs would a dangerous animal. Only this animal smelled good, warm and male, with a hint of honest sweat. She actually appreciated the scent of clean, masculine perspiration.

Better not to think about that.

She looked around the narrow basin with its sharp outcrops and natural protection. Good a place as any to stop. She dropped her knapsack, the forty pounds of gear thudding heavily against soggy, snow-patched earth.

"Do you want a fire?" she asked. Her eyes flicked to his and then away. There was something unnerving in looking into a man's eyes, as if she could read his soul, or worse that he could read hers.

"Wouldn't hurt to rest a bit, warm up, have something hot." North tossed his own knapsack beside a boulder as if the bag was empty. "Your nose is red."

Her hand went to her face, self-conscious that he would notice. She seldom considered her looks, and the fact that he made her do so, annoyed her. The fact that she noticed his annoyed her even more.

He was ruggedly good-looking. This morning he'd broken protocol and arrived unshaven. She wondered why.

"Pull an all-nighter last night, North?" she blurted.

Scraping together twigs for a fire, John didn't look up. "As a matter of fact, I did. Had one heck of a time."

Okay, she'd asked for that. Now she wondered exactly what an all-nighter entailed for John North. He didn't seem the type for wild parties, but what did she really know about him?

She couldn't resist prying. "Was it worth it?"

He responded with a scoffing noise that had both dogs tilting their heads, ears cocked.

"A barrel of laughs." He held a hand three feet off the ground. "Paperwork. A stack about this high. Being out here in the woods doesn't get my office job done."

A man without sleep was a danger to everyone. She knew that for a terrifying fact. "How much sleep did you get?"

Brown eyes drifted over her face. "About the same as you, I'd guess."

She bristled. "Was that an insult?"

His gaze flicked up to hers and then down to the fire where his cupped hands nursed a fledgling spark. "I'm not here to give you a hard time. Hand me some more dry wood."

It was an order, softly given, but an order just the same. She considered refusing, but because a fire was necessary for her benefit as well as the dogs, Melody did as he asked. Then she began the simple process of preparing warm, energizing food and drink. To hike for any length of time required frequent rest and nourishment.

Fingers stinging and clumsy from the cold, she stripped off her gloves and knelt in front of the fire. Nearby, an enormous flock of grosbeaks dipped and soared, clattering noisily in resentment of human intrusion. The dogs didn't react to the birds, were trained not to, and Melody was proud of them for remembering. Both sat near the campfire, tongues lolling, waiting for lunch.

On his haunches, John North lifted Chili's paws, examining each one. "This pad is getting raw. Better get a bootie on him."

Melody prickled. "I take care of my dogs."

John gently lowered Chili's paw and stared at her, silent. One of his wide, capable hands rested on Chili's head. The dog watched him with complete trust.

A seed of guilt took root in Melody's gut. She hated feeling guilty. That's why she didn't like people. They always made her feel things.

"Thanks," she said grudgingly and turned toward her pack to dig out the bootie. Chili watched with smiling eyes while she slipped paw protectors over his feet. Melody ruffled the Lab's ears and kissed his forehead.

The silence extended, compounding Melody's guilt. Her social contacts were mostly limited to dog trials and certifications. Being forced into the daily company of another person, particularly a man like North, made her realize how rusty her people skills had become.

Not that she cared all that much, but the man hadn't harmed her in any way. Yet.

Melody poured herself a cup of hot tomato soup and then as a peace offering, handed the tin mug to North. She shouldn't have snapped at him about the bootie.

"Thanks," John said, watching her, expression mild as though he recognized her attempt to apologize. By now, he'd settled back against a well-placed rock. He looked relaxed and

comfortable but capable and alert, too, an interesting combination. "How's the German shepherd doing?"

North had been there the day she'd taken Ace to Boulder for
surgery, had even offered to go along, though she'd turned him
down flat. He'd been kind to her dog that day, kind to her, too.
The dogs liked him. That was reassuring, if only incrementally.

"The surgery went well."

"When is he coming home?" The border collie sidled up
and stuck her pretty head beneath North's arm. Absently, as
though accustomed to insistent dogs, he scratched her ears,
then offered her a tidbit from his Power Bar. With dainty
manners, she took the morsel of peanut butter and oats
between her teeth and carried it a few paces away where she
lay down and munched.

"A couple more days."

"I guess you'll need some time off to drive up to Boulder."

"I guess." She found a comfortable spot as far away from
North as possible, a propitious spot where she could observe
his every move. The heat from the warm soup seeped from
her mouth to her stomach and outward, breaking the chill,
renewing her flagging energy.

"Take whatever time you need. The dog is important." His
whisker-rimmed lips softened, almost smiled. "The mountains aren't going anywhere."

Melody noticed the way his mouth moved, an uncomfortable jitter settling low in her belly. She forced her gaze to the
dogs.

"Ace is a special dog."

John sipped at his cup, his dark eyes quietly watching her.

"You miss him." It was a statement, not a question, as if
this disturbing man understood.

She swallowed, brushed an imaginary hair from her eyes. "Yes."

The fire popped, sending sparks high. John turned his attention there, watching. The sparks flamed briefly and died quietly on the wet snow.

"How did he get hurt?"

Melody ran a finger around the rim of the cup.

"An avalanche rescue. Ace fell into a crevice." Her mouth twisted in mixed emotion, remembering that bittersweet day. "But he found the father and son in time. I was so proud of him. Though badly injured, he wouldn't leave the scene until the victims were safe."

"How does that work when the dog is injured?" John tilted to one side, elbow on the rock, long body stretched out before the fire like a snake warming in the sun. "Is he airlifted with the victims?"

"Usually, but Ace was too distraught. I couldn't let them take him away from me."

"What did you do?" His fingers fidgeted with a twig but his focus was on her. There was something about his fingers that drew her. She recalled the feel of that one strong hand holding hers against his belly. Disconcerting. He was a most disconcerting man.

She twitched a shoulder. "I carried him."

"But he weighs seventy or eighty pounds, easy."

"Eighty-five." A tiny proud smile pushed at her lips. Her strength and stamina surprised him. Good. He needed to know she was strong. "I'd do it again in a heartbeat."

"Pretty special animal."

"He is. At least to me." She blew across the top of her soup before downing the remainder.

"And to the people he saved that night, too." He tossed the twig into the fire and brushed his hands down the leg of his pants. "Will he be able to work again?"

"We're optimistic."

"He deserves the chance."

She tilted her head in agreement. This was the first real conversation Melody had allowed with the man. And she found the experience, if not pleasant, at least not awful.

She was contemplating that curious turn of events, distracted enough to take her eyes off him for a second.

It was a mistake.

John North was around the fire and had his hand over her mouth before she could scream.

CHAPTER FIVE

"Not a sound," John whispered, suddenly transported to another time and place. A place of imminent danger.

A fierce protective urge pounded through him like machine-gun fire. He pressed Melody closer, arms around her, his body between her and the danger.

Somewhere in the back of his mind was the knowledge that he liked the way she felt. That her body curved, her cheek was velvet, her scent fresh and enticing. Later. He'd think of that later. Afterward.

Hackles stood stiff on the dogs' backs. A low growl emanated from Chili. He, too, wanted to protect Melody.

John kept his eyes on the danger above them on the ledge, praying the fire would drive it away.

"Stay calm," he commanded, slowly taking his hand from her mouth, "and calm the dogs."

Again his voice was quieter than death, a mere sigh on the wind.

For one frozen moment, Melody obeyed.

And then she came unglued.

A sharp elbow caught him in the gut. Air woofed from

him. He relaxed his hold and cursed himself for a fool. Any Ranger knew better than to let his guard down.

Melody spun away, cat's eyes wide and furious. She fought, kicking out, swinging her arms, connecting with his thick clothes. He caught her wrist, warding off blow after blow.

She was a wild thing, completely unexpected. What was wrong with this woman?

Behind him Chili growled deep in his throat. John had the fleeting thought that, at any moment, the dog could go for the lion or for him. Either way was not good.

"Melody. Stop," he managed between punches. "I'm not trying to hurt you. There's a cougar. *A cougar.*"

The next swing died in midair. "What?"

"A mountain lion. On the overhang above."

Wild-eyed, panting, she swung around, looked up. "Where? I don't see anything."

John spun, too. The cat was gone. "Our noise and movements must have frightened him off."

She looked at him, eyes narrowed in suspicion. If she hadn't been shaking so hard, the suspicion would have angered him. He wasn't accustomed to having his motives questioned.

The dogs moved in between them then, tails between their legs, whining softly. Hair stood up on their backs. They'd been trained to pay no attention to wild animals, but the big cat had gotten their attention.

Melody went to her knees, visibly trembling. She stroked each dog in turn. "They're spooked. Maybe there *was* a cougar."

John's jaw hardened. "There was. I saw it. He was there on the ledge, crouched, ready to pounce."

Her gaze flew up to his. "On us?"

"That's the way it looked to me. Probably aiming for one

of the dogs." He knelt beside her, wanting to touch her in apology, but worried she'd go off again. "I'm sorry if I scared you."

She sidled away. Her reply caught him off guard. "You've been in the military, haven't you?"

He sat back on his haunches, searching her face, puzzled by the abrupt, out-of-context question. "Army Rangers, thirteen years. Where did that come from?"

Melody regarded him cautiously. Something deep and bewildering swam in the silver depths of those bizarre eyes. She hadn't liked him before and probably never would now. And he still had no idea why. All he'd done was try to protect her.

What a joke. Melody needed his protection about as much as Colorado needed more mountains.

"Military." Jaw tight, her chin bobbed. "That's what I thought. Stealth and attack, no one sees it coming."

He narrowed his eyes at the indictment in her tone.

"What are you? One of those bleeding hearts that hate the military and consider us all baby killers?"

He'd killed a few people, but they'd all been bad guys. Not that he was proud of that fact, but he'd saved a lot of babies in the process. He *was* proud of that, though he'd come away with his share of scars and nightmares. A man didn't take the loss of life lightly and he'd left too many comrades behind.

Melody shook her head and pushed to her feet. Her face was pale and her hands unsteady as she began tossing supplies into her backpack. "Never mind. We need to get moving. It's going to snow."

He grabbed her arm to stop the frenzied movements. "I don't think so. Not until we talk. What just happened here?"

Her gaze dropped to where his fingers wrapped around her biceps. "Please remove your hand."

"Not until you explain some things."

"I owe you nothing."

The chill in her tone sliced him like a razor. He dropped his hand. "True enough, but I owe you."

The switch caught her off guard. She stood, breath rapid, the scent of fear flowing from her in waves, glaring at him with enough animosity to start a forest fire. What had he done? Why had she reacted so violently?

He glared back, trying to read her and coming away empty.

Maybe she wasn't worth the trouble. He should give it up and do this job alone. Who needed a prickly, angry, suspicious partner in the dangerous mountain wilderness?

He raked a hand up the back of his neck and squeezed. Who was he kidding? She was indispensable. He'd grown up in these mountains but during his long stint in the army everything had changed so much. He would need years to learn the things and places she already knew. Her experience and expertise far surpassed his.

Besides, something told him her attitude was an outward shell developed for protection, though from what, he couldn't imagine. Most of the time, they worked companionably, or at least he thought so. They talked little, but he was accustomed to quiet on a mission. A blabbermouth would drive him nuts.

She was exceptionally kind to her dogs, seeing to their needs before her own. She never complained about the long hours or the rough terrain. She never complained of hunger or cold or fatigue. She simply worked, earning her meager pay a thousand times over.

John relented. His mama always said he could catch more

flies with honey than with vinegar. Though he never understand why anyone would want to catch flies, he figured the
adage applied in Melody's case.

"Thank you for your help up here," he said. Though grati-
tude was hard to express on the heels of her fury, John meant
every word. In special forces, he'd learned to control his own
emotions when the opponent didn't. He'd also learned to do
whatever it took to accomplish the mission, regardless of his
own feelings. "I don't know if I've told you before, but I'm
grateful. I couldn't make this happen without you. Your expertise is going to save lives."

The steam went out of her then. Her throat worked as
though she wanted to say more. Her eyelashes, killer long and
coal-black, though she didn't wear mascara, fluttered. Not a
flirtatious flutter—though the male in him wondered what
flirting with her would be like—but a flutter of confusion.

She swallowed hard and nodded. "Better get moving."

Then with jerky, mechanical movements she began to clean
up the camp.

Hands on hips, he watched her for a minute and then began
his own cleanup.

Melody Crawford didn't trust him any farther than she
could throw this mountain.

And John North took that as a personal challenge.

By day five, John thought they might be making progress.
Anyway, Melody talked to him more. Nothing personal, just
the usual chitchat. Yet, she still walked behind him, still
watched him with those strange, suspicious eyes, still bristled
if he got too close.

He adjusted the pack on his back and with it, adjusted his

train of thought. He had a lot more to worry about today than his skittish partner.

"I can't work on this project tomorrow," he said. Though she trailed along behind him, she was close. He could feel her there. "The office work is piling up. Even working weekends and nights I can't keep up."

"I can continue the work up here without you."

He was afraid she'd say that. They'd come to a high ridge, with an incline shooting down like a giant slide covered with loose, gravelly talus. He stopped, hands on hips to survey the area. Cloud cover cast long shadows over the rugged terrain. Melody walked up beside him. Her diminutive form was considerably shorter than his six feet.

He slanted a look in her direction. In profile she was pretty and soft-looking. Only when she turned and aimed those chilling eyes at him did she appear wary and tough.

"Isn't tomorrow the day you spring Ace from the hospital?"

Her mouth curved. She had a great mouth. A few times he'd wondered what she'd do if he kissed it. He figured he knew and the thought wasn't pretty. He still bore a purple bruise on his shin from one of her kicks.

The thought brought a grin. Spunky, tough girl. He didn't know why, but Melody was a challenge he couldn't back down from.

"Tomorrow's the day," she said. "I can't wait to see him."

She removed one of her gloves and slid her reddened fingers beneath her sweatshirt. John was tempted to offer the inside of his jacket for her use. He wouldn't mind warming her fingers—or any of her other parts for that matter.

He frowned at the wayward thoughts. What was wrong with him today?

"I'll take off tomorrow, too, and work in the office," he said. "Probably the rest of the week. There have been some problems."

She shifted toward him and again, his thoughts misbehaved. "What's wrong?"

"Ah, I missed a meeting yesterday. The weird thing is I didn't even know about it, but the council was ticked." And positive PR was essential to the longevity of his department. If he was perceived as doing a poor job, he'd be out on his ear at year's end. The truth of that was enough to rein in any thoughts of his intriguing partner.

"I don't get it. Why would they be upset if you hadn't been informed?"

"That's the problem. They claimed to have sent a written invitation, followed by a phone message. I don't remember getting either one."

One eyebrow twitched. "Losing your memory, Ranger?"

"If I am, the loss is extremely selective."

He'd gone over and over in his mind, but the information was not there. Someone else must have taken the message when he was out and forgotten to give it to him. And maybe the written invitation was somewhere at the bottom of a pile of papers. He had plenty of those.

"Hazardous incline," he said, turning his attention to the here and now. The other would wait until tomorrow, though he was glad there had been no emergencies this week. He'd wanted to get a good start on this grid project, then taper off, working part-time on the project and the rest of the time on other duties. Currently, he was spread pretty thin. "We could avoid this area, take a different route."

"There's an old primitive cabin farther on. I say we cross

here and map that area. It's just the sort of place a lost hunter or hiker might stumble upon for shelter."

"Can't argue that. Come on. You first." He offered a hand to steady her descent.

She drew away, one hand up in a stop sign. "I can manage."

"I know you can. Humor me." John raised his arms in a shrug. "I'm a guy. If I let you fall, my image will be smashed to heck."

She made a funny noise in the back of her throat. John could almost swear she wanted to laugh. "Oh, be honest. If anything happens to me, you lose your wilderness guide."

Her eyebrows lifted in slight amusement, the first time she'd ever teased him.

A smile bloomed in his chest. Yep. Progress.

He snapped his fingers in mock resignation. "Dang. You figured out my ulterior motive. So, now you have to protect my fragile ego and let me assist you." Feet braced wide apart on the slope, he reached back toward her. "Toss your bag down."

She did as he said, surprisingly without argument for once. Maybe they were getting somewhere. He was anxious to win her trust though he couldn't say why, other than the obvious. Partners trusted each other, watched each other's back, were there for each other when the going got rough.

She'd been kidding about her importance as his guide, but John figured Melody Crawford would be extremely valuable in a real crisis.

When she grasped his outstretched hand, John experienced a measure of victory. Maybe his ego *did* need stoking. He tightened his muscles, determined not to let her fall.

With her free hand, Melody jabbed a trekking pole into the hard surface for extra security, but halfway down the skid took over and the pole bounced down without her. John, who'd scaled mountains and cliffs in Afghanistan carrying a seventy-five-pound pack and a rifle, jockeyed for balance, expecting to find it. He didn't.

They both lost control at the same time. Boots grated as their feet slid out from under them. They went down hard and finished the journey on their bottoms and backs, landing in separate heaps along a wet creek bed.

As soon as John's boots thudded against solid ground, he sprang upright. "Are you all right?"

He rushed to Melody's side and touched her shoulder. She rolled away and up, laughing. "That was fun."

Hands on hips, John stepped back and laughed, as much with relief that she was all right as with amusement at her reaction. "Yeah, it was."

This kind of adrenaline high had kept him a Ranger for all those years. The quest for adventure, particularly the uncertain, the treacherous, revved his engine.

"Want to do it again?" she asked.

Apparently, Melody Crawford was a kindred spirit.

He grinned, admiring her rosy cheeks and pink nose as much as her adventuresome spirit. "I have a feeling we'll have to at some point."

Melody held his gaze, lips tilted.

The dogs skidded down the incline, too, but unlike the humans, arrived on all four feet, tongues lolling, eyes alight with the fun of the ride. They danced around Melody's feet, eager for her attention. She didn't disappoint. Going to one knee, she ruffled fur and murmured unintelligible praise. She was different with the animals. Her guard was down all the time, much as it had been in the last few minutes with him. In the dogs' company, she was softened, gentle, her claws sheathed.

With a thoughtful smile, John watched the trio. "I just have one question, oh mighty wilderness guide."

"What's that?" She glanced up. And darn if his gut didn't react to the fun in her expression.

"How are we going to get back up?"

Her pleasure turned to puzzlement, and then she burst out laughing again. The sound was musical, as pretty as bird-song, just as it had been the morning he'd surprised her at the cabin.

"You should do that more often," he said, studying her face, watching those eyes shift from silver to gold in the sunlight, enjoying the play of pleasure on her face. The lightness in his belly expanded.

"Do what?" she asked, grinning. "Fall down a mountain?"

He reached to brush the shaggy bangs from her eyes. "Laugh."

"Oh." She turned her head then, breaking contact so that he was forced to drop his hand.

She leaped to her feet, and brushed the dirt and rocks from her bottom. It was a nice bottom, though he wished he wouldn't notice. But notice he did. This rugged outdoors-woman looked curvy and feminine in her ski suits and jeans. He wondered if she knew she was sexy. Probably not.

When she turned, the smile was gone, and her guard was up again.

"Move it, North. Daylight's waning." She hoisted her backpack and started off.

So much for progress.

The next day Melody drove to Boulder and brought Ace home to the cabin. Her old buddy had lost weight, a fact that chipped away at her already battered heart. But he was standing and walking on those repaired knees, a miracle to both him and her.

Chili was ecstatic but cautiously sniffed Ace's knees as if he understood his partner couldn't play yet.

"Six or eight weeks, Chili. Be patient."

Loading her with instructions for the dog's care and proper rehab, the vets were confident Ace could work again. She was deliriously happy to hear it, so much so that she almost wished for someone to share the good news. There was no one. Her living relatives were distant and wouldn't care anyway. Granny Perkins had been the only one who understood her need for the dogs and for solitude.

John North invaded her mind as he did too often of late. As always, she pushed him away.

Once Ace was settled, Melody placed the bag of medication and instructions on the table and took out the bill.

She'd paid with a newly acquired credit card and, even now, her stomach knotted with the knowledge that she was in debt up to her ears. As long as her new job and her nerves held out, she could make the payments.

Yesterday's trek with John had been easier for some reason, maybe because of the tumble she and her boss had taken. John North seemed less intimidating, less military, almost gentle at times. And he liked her laugh.

She went into the bedroom and stood in front of the old cheval mirror that had come with the house. The object looked out of place here in the simple, rustic cabin, a piece of feminine frippery. But she liked the oval shape and the smooth, glossy mahogany frame.

She pushed her bangs back from her forehead, remembering the feel of John North's fingers on her skin when he'd done the same. Why had he touched her that way? She didn't like people to take liberties with her person. It made her uncomfortable.

But she remembered just the same. There had been tenderness in him. A hard military man with tenderness. She couldn't quite reconcile the incongruity.

In the slant of weak sunlight coming in through the window, the tiny scar gleamed white and ugly.

Had the sharply observant John North seen the scar?

With a shiver, she released her hair. The bangs fell forward again, covering the past.

She touched her ears. Once a long time ago, before the nightmare, she'd had them pierced. Back then, she'd loved pretty things, dangly earrings, shiny bracelets. How long had it been since she'd worn a pair of earrings?

Removing her town clothes, as she called those items reserved for trips into civilization, she remained in front of the mirror, taking stock. She pressed the heels of her hands down her sides, over her hips. Her body was fit and taut, thanks to her work with the dogs. But the woman who looked back at her was ordinary, plain even, except for the strange cat eyes that had caused more than one person to make rude remarks.

Not that she cared. She wasn't attractive and didn't want to be. The less people noticed her, the more they left her alone.

But she couldn't help wondering what kind of woman appealed to John North. Surely, he had women. A man that good-looking and masculine always had women.

She made a noise of self-derision. She didn't even like John North. What did she care about his women?

"Stupid," she said to the petite figure in the mirror and then went to the narrow closet for her outdoor gear.

The dogs had yet to be exercised and there was training to be done.

She was pulling on her boots when the telephone rang. Probably the vet checking on Ace. Proud of his surgical work and a man who loved animals, he'd promised to do that.

The boot thumped against the hardwood of her kitchen floor as she headed to the bedroom to answer the only phone in the house. "Hello."

"Hey. How's Ace doing?" A deceptively soft baritone caressed her ear.

Her stomach took a nosedive. It wasn't the vet. It was John North.

"Good, I think. He's lost weight but he's happy to be home."

"He missed you." Just that simple declaration caused a curl of pleasure as bright and lovely as birthday ribbon. "Can he walk?"

"Better than he could and the vet says his strength and flexibility will improve every day. He has to do special exercises."

"He must be doing well. You sound happy."

The ribbon of pleasure stretched higher, turning her lips up into a smile. "Ecstatic. Oh, John, I think he's going to do really well. They're sure he'll work again and I am, too."

"Good. Good."

A quiet hum ensued. Melody searched for words to say. She was horrible at conversation, but she wasn't ready to break connection. In the background, Melody heard a door close and then the sound of paper shuffling.

"Are you in the office?"

"Yes, ma'am. Up to my ears." The quiet answer carried an element of amused self-mockery. John North wasn't a man who took himself too seriously.

"How is it going?" She stopped short of saying she'd missed him today. Had she? Maybe. She wasn't sure. She pressed the receiver closer to her ear. "Are you back in the council's good graces yet?"

"I've been kissing up a little, making calls. Took the mayor to lunch."

"Any clue what happened?"

"I have an idea, but no evidence. I never found the invitation so if it arrived in this office, someone else opened it."

She knew he was a one-man office, so a harried secretary wasn't to blame. "That sounds ominous. Do you think someone deliberately hid the messages from you?"

"I wish I didn't."

"But you do."

"Yes, ma'am, I do."

"Why? Why would anyone want to make you look bad?"

"Everyone has enemies, I guess. Hard to believe, I know, since I'm such a lovable guy."

She laughed. And when she did, he chuckled.

"Do it again," he said.

"Do what again?"

"Laugh. You're cheering me up."

She remembered then. He liked her laugh. She grew self-conscious, also remembering that a man like him was bound to have women.

"Don't you have someone at home to cheer you up?" She wished she hadn't asked, but there it was. Hopefully, he wouldn't read anything into the casual question.

"Nobody at home but me. Not even a dog."

"You don't have a dog?" She transferred her odd feeling

of relief to incredulity. "You must remedy that situation. Everyone needs a dog."

She pressed the receiver between her shoulder and ear, walking around the room as they talked. It was a habit she couldn't break, always moving, even on the telephone. Using a ragged sock, she began dusting the sparse furniture.

"Eventually, I'll get one. I've been looking."

"Maybe the next time you go into Denver for one of your meetings, you can visit the shelter."

"You'd have to go along to make sure I pick the right mongrel."

Melody leaned an elbow against the ancient dresser in her bedroom, dusting around the odds and ends she'd cast aside on its scarred top. "Hmm, I don't think so."

"Ah, come on. Why not? A trip to Denver, get a dog. I might even spring for dinner."

She shook her head, aware he couldn't see the motion. Dread replaced the pleasure.

She picked up the framed photo on her dresser and stared at the smiling family.

She'd lived in Denver. She'd also died in Denver.

Here on top of the world, alone with her dogs, she was safe. Better keep it that way.

CHAPTER SIX

JOHN SHOOK ONE LAST HAND at the Rotary Club, finishing up the talk on the progress of the Emergency Management Department and the need for more volunteers. He'd been well received and the luncheon meeting had given him an escape from his tiny, cramped office. He was going stir-crazy, the old urge to be outside crawling up his spine like spiders, demanding attention.

A week had passed since he'd be out in the field. A week since he and Melody had backpacked into the wilderness.

She was making progress without him, but John didn't like the fact that she was working alone any more than he liked being stuck in the office so long. No one should hike the mountain wilderness alone and as her employer he was responsible if something happened to her on the job. Never mind that she lived and worked alone all the time. He preferred she not do it on his watch.

He stepped out into the parking lot, lifted his face to the sky. A light snow fell. Yesterday, it had rained. Such was spring in the Rockies.

He wondered if Melody was out today. He'd told her to take no chances. She'd laughed at him. He figured the injury to his sense of command was worth getting to hear that laugh of hers.

Okay, so he missed her. If missing a porcupine was possible.

Nah, that wasn't fair. She could be bristly, but he'd been in the military with men far more sharp-edged and intense than Melody. And he'd trusted them with his life. Underneath those thorns was a complicated woman with the capacity for great tenderness. He'd stake his Silver Star on it. That's why she intrigued him. To his way of thinking, she was buried treasure. What would she be like if she ever let go of the rigid control?

Fascinating question.

He'd also discovered another interesting fact about Miss Melody Crawford. On the telephone she was different, as if the distance allowed her to be more relaxed.

On his order, she checked in every night with the day's progress. And if the conversations lasted far longer than business, so what? There was the recuperating dog to discuss. And his job. She always asked about his work, always listened with a pithy comment. She was witty. And smart. And he was smart enough to listen to her mountain wisdom.

They were partners, too. They had the project in common. She was useful to him. And he was a man, alive and well and long without a woman. That's all there was to missing her. He needed more of a social life.

In the army a man learned to keep his urges sublimated. But he wasn't in the army anymore.

Still, there was no one in Glass Falls who stirred his interest. Right now he was too busy to become embroiled in a relationship, anyway.

Melody's ski-suit-clad body and wild, rock star haircut flashed in his head. He snorted and shook away the image.

Eager to get out of town, he started his 4X4 and headed to the store for a few supplies. Once inside, he gathered some odds and ends and made a beeline for the checkout counter, anxious to let the serenity of the wilderness drain away the stresses of life.

He thumped a pack of his favorite granola snacks, some peanut butter and crackers along with packs of dry soup and hot chocolate mix onto the counter next to batteries and dog treats. Ace was fond of beef jerky.

While waiting for the cashier to ring up the sale, John turned for a look at the candy display. His sweet tooth was working overtime lately. He wondered which kind Melody would like.

The cashier was a bleached blonde with black eyebrows and a friendly demeanor who chatted him up every time he came in. Today was no different.

"So, how is our new local hero doing?" she asked. It was the same thing she said every time.

"Not feeling too heroic, but I can't complain."

The scanner beeped as she slid merchandise along the counter with one hand and poked at the cash register with the other. "That's good. I'd heard things were a little rocky for the new department. Sure would hate to lose it."

"Rocky? Who told you that?"

"Mmm." She paused and rolled her eyes toward her eyebrows as though the name was written there. "Not sure. Someone said you were having trouble keeping up, you'd missed some important meetings, the mayor wasn't happy, I don't remember the details. Maybe it was the mayor's wife I talked to." She shook her head. "I told her a one-man office can't do everything. You need some help."

He appreciated the vote of confidence, from her at least. Apparently not everyone shared the sentiment. "I'm keeping up. And I only missed one meeting. One. Someone forgot to let me know about it."

"Well, I hope someone told you about Glass Creek."

He tensed. "What about Glass Creek?"

"A fisherman was in yesterday, said the creek was really high, nearing flood stage."

This was news to him. "Did you tell him to call my office?"

"Well, I may have told him to call the sheriff's office. Old habits die hard, but he said he would." She pushed the total key. "Twenty-three, seventy-six is your total. Last time, the spring floods hit us, I had four inches of water in my living room. You'll check it out, won't you?"

She took his money, dispensed change, all the while relating the horrors of the last flood. John had been concerned about Glass Creek for some time, but this latest information was new. Thankfully, he already had an evacuation plan in place and volunteers ready to sandbag.

But he'd been in his office all day yesterday. Why hadn't he received the fisherman's report?

It was late afternoon by the time Melody and John reached the area above Glass Creek. Worried about flooding, John had been adamant about gridding this section today, which was not far from the spot where they'd seen the cougar. Rather, where John claimed to have seen the cougar. Melody had thought long and hard about that episode, still wondering if there had truly been a mountain lion on the ridge. John had frightened her, no doubt about that. For a minute, she thought he'd lost it, gone berserk. But considering how quickly he'd snapped out of guerrilla mode, and having no other explanation for his behavior, she'd resolved to believe him.

"We're going to have to make it a short day," John said,

casting a glance overhead. The wind was up and gray clouds gathered off to the west. "Maybe another couple of hours before we start back down."

They'd parked John's 4X4 at the trailhead and hiked a good three miles into the dark spruce backcountry. These areas off the beaten track were where visitors could easily become disoriented and lost.

Melody studied the sky in silence. A storm was brewing. But in this unpredictable land, the weather might break in the next five minutes or wait until tonight.

John North knew that as well as she did, so Melody said nothing. In fact, she'd prefer not to talk to him at all. He was messing with her head.

Her stupid heart had leaped into her throat when John's truck pulled into her yard this afternoon. The emotion was not welcome. Why should she be glad to see him?

Maybe she was starting to like him. Maybe that was the problem. He made her feel things. Things she didn't want to feel.

She'd begun looking forward to their nightly phone conversations, so much so that she spent half the afternoon thinking of things to tell him.

Stupid. Dangerous.

Annoyed, she stabbed the trekking poles hard against the earth and leaned on them while using the tiny computer. The land was rugged here, treacherous even, and the cliffs and ridges numerous. Somewhere ahead was a lake surrounded by towering pine and snow-kissed rock faces shooting hundreds of feet into the sky. She hoped to make it there. Staring into the mirrored face of an unnamed lake, surrounded by nothing but nature and quiet, refreshed her spirit.

John North understood that, too. She'd watched him pause on a ridge in near reverence to stare down into a lush valley. She'd seen him lift his face to the sky and watch a pair of hawks catch the currents. She'd even heard his sigh of contentment when a doe and fawn gazed back at him across a meadow.

Like her, John North loved the mountains. Maybe that's why she sort of liked him. Sometimes.

"Look up there," John said, pointing high above to a precipice where the spiked horns of a mountain goat glinted in the sun.

Chili had spotted the animal, too, and stood rigidly at attention. Nature made him want to give chase. Training kept him under control.

"It's only a goat," she groused, more in self-defense than irritation. She loved seeing any of nature's creatures, but with her thoughts of John North going crazy today, she needed to push him away.

John grinned as though he saw right through her.

How did she combat a man like that?

The goat ambled away as clouds began to gather. They were around eight thousand feet and the air held a tinge of moisture she recognized. Rain. Snow. Something was coming.

They approached a small stream, jotted the info on the computer and decided to travel upstream rather than cross and risk a soaking. Suddenly the wind shifted, picked up. Blue and purple clouds that had seemed faraway a while ago now boiled overhead.

A strong gust of cold air sent Melody staggering backward. "Whoa!"

John North spun around, his hair blowing straight back

from his face. Stalking toward her, he looked like a fierce
warrior god, able to control the elements.

"Storm's coming," he said, uselessly. "Head for the truck."

"We won't make it." She'd no more than said the words
when the sky lit up. Thunder crashed, echoing loudly from
one mountain to another. Ferocious lightning ripped the
heavens and the skies opened. A sudden torrent of cold rain
sucked the breath from her. As if someone had dumped a tub
of water from above, they were drenched in seconds.

"We have to find shelter," John shouted, taking her arm.
Water ran from his face and clothes. Though he stood directly
in front of her, she could barely see him, barely hear him. The
sound around them was deafening.

"The cabin we saw yesterday. It's our best bet," he shouted
into her face.

She nodded. Here in the open was the worst place they
could be. More people were killed in the mountains by lightning than anything else.

The cabin, if they could get there without being struck, was
not that far.

A jagged bolt of electricity slammed the earth not thirty
feet away. Dirt shot into the air. They both jumped. John po-
sitioned his body in an arch over hers.

For a fraction of time, Melody felt protected.

He reached for her backpack, slipped it off her shoulders
before she could argue and slung it over his arm. "Run!"

She did. But even with two bags to carry, John North
moved quickly ahead like a stealth bomber, fast and powerful.

The storm raged around them, both terrifying and beautiful in its power. Hail pelted down, a little at first and then like
golf balls gone crazy.

Melody's lungs ached, and rain obscured her vision. Chili stayed at her side, bless him, the only dog she'd brought today. Poor guy, he hated lightning.

As she reached the crooked steps of the cabin, a jarring bolt of lightning crashed so near, she yelped and dived toward the door.

Strong hands yanked her inside. Chili streaked past.

Melody collapsed on her knees on the floor, panting and shivering with cold. Her ears rang.

John North crouched in front of her. Water sluiced from his clothes to puddle around his feet. "You okay?"

She pushed sodden hair from her eyes and grinned, breathless. Her adrenaline-juiced pulse still thundered like the storm. "Was that fun, or what?"

John rocked back and laughed. "You are a different kind of woman."

Chili chose that moment to rid his sodden coat of excess water, showering them both. John tried to duck and tipped sideways in the process. It was Melody's turn to laugh.

Making a wry face, John righted himself and began to bivouac. "We need a fire fast. It's too cold to stay wet. We'll be hypothermic in minutes."

Melody shivered and rubbed at her upper arms. "Won't argue that."

The cabin was little more than a hunter's shack with one room, which, lucky for them, held a rough rock fireplace and a few sticks of gathered wood, though not much else. "At least we can get dry and warm."

"This storm may last half the night," he said, his back to her so he didn't see the reaction his declaration caused. "If it does, we're stuck here."

No way was she spending the night in one room with him.

"We'll make it back to the truck," she insisted. "This will let up." She hoped.

"I wouldn't count on it." He was so casual, so unconcerned, while her insides rioted.

"I'm not staying here."

John shifted, his wet boots squeaking on the dirty wood floor. His quiet eyes drilled into her, unyielding. "I'm in charge of this project. For safety's sake, you'll do as I say."

Every cell in her body reacted. Hair raised on the back of her neck. Goose bumps that had nothing to do with the chill covered her arms.

"Big news, tough guy. I don't do authority well."

His look was mildly amused. "Now, why does that not surprise me?"

"So don't tell me what I will or will not do."

He stalked to the door, throwing it open. Chili bolted for a corner. "Take off then, Miss Independence."

A powerful gust whipped through the opening in a wet sheet. Hail rattled the porch and bounced into the shack. Lightning sizzled and crackled, lighting up the sky with ferocious power.

He was right, darn it. No one was safe out in that. They were stuck here until the storm passed. She only hoped it would pass quickly. Traveling in the dark she could handle, but even she was cautious in lightning storms.

"You've made your point. Shut the door."

To his credit, North didn't smirk in victory. He quietly shut out the storm and returned to the fireplace.

"Since you don't take orders well, may I politely request you find us something hot to drink?" he said, just a hint of wicked humor glinting from brown eyes.

The humor got to her. "You may. Would you prefer soup, coffee or hot chocolate?"

"Anything. Just don't poison me."

"Silly me. I forgot to bring my arsenic."

The fire caught, flamed up, bathing his skin in gold. Wood smoke fragranced with pine needles circled around him, scenting the room. The handful of dry wood wouldn't last long, but at least they could get warm and dry.

Outside, the sky had darkened and the meager fire also provided much-needed light. Even with that, the cabin's interior was dim and shadowy.

Melody's boots squished as she dumped her food supplies on the wobbly excuse for a table, one of exactly three pieces of furniture in the place, the other two being equally wobbly chairs. She took out her cookware, a spoon and a tin pot with matching cups.

John came up beside her, adding his backpack. His voice rumbled next to her ear. "Go ahead and take off your clothes."

The tin pot clattered to the floor. Melody's head jerked toward him.

John held up one hand but his eyes were dancing with devilment. "Wait. Let me rephrase. May I politely request that you remove your wet clothing? I plan to do the same."

He was standing so close she could hear him breathe and feel the heat of his body even through the wet clothes. A flush heated the back of her neck.

Something that wasn't fear, something rather pleasant hummed through her blood. She tamped it down.

They were both soaked to the skin. The request was sensible. A little embarrassing, maybe even titillating, but practical. She prided herself on practicality.

"Tell me you have dry clothes in your bag," she muttered around the thickness in her throat.

His mouth twitched. "What if I don't?"

She reached into her bag and yanked out a blanket. "Then you wear this."

She tossed the blanket to him. He caught it one-handed, holding the soft pink-and-red fleece up to the firelight.

"Ladybugs," he said, the corners of his mouth crinkling into a full-blown grin. "My color, too." He waggled his eyebrows. "Wanna share with me?"

"I don't share well, either."

"Life is cruel." He sighed and sat down on one of the chairs to unlace his boots.

She waited, still wondering if she'd have to spend the next several hours trying not to look at him wrapped in a pink blanket that wouldn't begin to cover all of him. When he didn't relieve her curiosity, she put water to heat over the fire and then removed her boots and jacket.

North's boots thumped to the floor. He peeled off his shirt.

Oh, my.

Melody's fingers froze on her bootlaces. She sucked in a lungful of smoke-scented air.

"Hey, wait a minute. A warning please."

He tossed the soggy shirt aside.

"Sorry." He was no such thing. "Afraid you'll lose control and want me?"

"I'm beside myself with passion." She shoved the discarded blanket at him.

His grin was unrepentant as he held the blanket in his teeth, letting the fleece material form an inverted cone of protection in front of him. But his wide shoulders and most of his naturally tanned and muscled chest remained stunningly visible. Melody turned away but not before the humming started in her blood again. And also not before she saw two scars—one on his left shoulder and another that puckered his right side.

"The pants are next," he warned, almost chuckling. "Sure you don't want to watch?"

"I'll try to control myself," she answered, her throat dry as salted crackers. Good lands. Alone with John North was bad enough. Alone with a naked, teasing John North was enough to make her insane.

Her hands stirred two cups of instant cocoa but her mind was acutely aware of every whisper of fabric, every shift and shuffle behind her. In the tiny room, a man of John's size and uncomfortable masculinity was overpowering.

"All done."

She almost wilted with relief. "Does that mean you're decent?"

"Depends on your definition."

Melody rolled her eyes heavenward. He was teasing, she kept telling herself. He was only having fun with her, showing off, flirting the way guys loved to do.

Flirting? At the thought, she jerked. Hot water splashed her hand. "Ow!"

She hurriedly set the pot aside and yanked the offended skin to her lips. Instantly, John was at her side, tugging the hand away from her mouth, studying the rising blister.

A shiver of something really, really nice danced along her nerve endings.

"I'm okay." She attempted to extract her hand from his. North was unrelenting. He held on, ministering to her as if she was helpless. He wrapped his cold, wet T-shirt around her palm. The relief was instant.

"Leave that on for a few minutes. The cold will help draw out the heat." He hovered, scanning her face as if truly concerned.

Melody didn't know how to react to this perplexing man. To a woman alone for more than fifteen years, John North and his kindness was as foreign as life on Mars.

"The hot chocolate is ready," she said, uncertain of what else to say. "I see you didn't need my blanket after all."

Still, John didn't move.

"No fun to be naked under a blanket without company." Indeed, he'd changed into a thermal shirt and loose flannel pants. "You'd better get changed, too. You're shivering."

There was more than one cause of those shivers. "Promise to turn your back?"

He emitted a beleaguered sigh.

"Spoilsport," he said, but he turned away and began organizing supplies on the tabletop.

For once, she had no choice. She had to trust him.

Melody made short work of the wet clothes, but she kept an eye on the tall, intimidating man only a few feet away. Her mind went crazy. What would she do if he turned around?

Was he as curious about her body as she was his?

At the notion, her fingers fumbled on a zipper. Okay, so she was curious. She'd admit that much.

True to his word, John kept his back turned until Melody announced, "I'm dressed."

John executed an about-face. The dancing flames of the fire cast light and shadows over his crooked grin. "Darn, and I was hoping to catch you naked."

She threw a wet shirt at him. He laughed and went back to

his task, but his words echoed in her head for a long time. Maybe he *was* curious. Or maybe he was just a man who liked to tease.

The dog lay stretched in front of the fire, waiting for dinner, a good excuse to get busy and get her mind off John North and being naked. Melody fed and watered Chili first and then prepared a simple meal for her and her troublesome partner. Meanwhile, John fashioned a clothesline from rappelling rope and spread their wet items out to dry. All the while, Melody prayed the storm would pass. It didn't.

With the meal over, there was little to do but wait and stay warm. Melody was acutely aware of the efficient way John North moved around the shack. He was restless, as she was.

"The storm is not letting up," he said, turning from the window. "And it's getting dark."

Her heart sank into her thermal socks. The dark didn't bother her. She worked in the darkness all the time. The storm was a different matter. "We're stuck here."

"I've been stuck in worse places," he said. Considering his military career, she imagined he had. "And with worse company."

The last was offered with a smile.

"You can't be too sure about that," she said. "Maybe I'm as witchy as some people think. Or spooky or crazy or whatever it is they say about me."

"I hope you won't let stupid remarks get to you."

"I am what I am. No excuses." But the remarks hurt. She pulled a wobbly chair away from the small table and sat. "I hope Ace is okay."

John took one of the other chairs and straddled it backward, resting his arms along the top. The move was an entirely masculine action. No female she'd ever known sat like that.

"I hadn't thought about your other dogs. Do they have food and water?"

"I fed them this morning. And they always have water available, but Ace will worry." He was healthy enough to let himself in and out of the doggy door but she didn't like the idea of him being outside alone.

"Nothing we can do about it. No signal on the cell phone."

"Doesn't matter. Ace isn't allowed to answer the phone when I'm not there anyway."

John tilted his head in appreciation of the joke. "Cute. But you know what I mean. We can't inform anyone of our where-abouts."

"That's the reason I don't own a cell phone." Other than finances. "They never work when you need them."

"So here we are," he said, radiating false cheer. "No TV, no radio, no nothing but each other and one wet, stinky dog. Might as well talk."

"About what?"

He lifted a finger in a mini imitation of a shrug. "Whatever. Let's start with you. Any family out there worrying about you?"

"No."

"Nobody?"

The images flickered behind her eyes, far back in the dark places inside her memory.

"Not a living soul."

"That's crappy. Everyone needs family. It's tough to lose people you care about."

"I guess you've been there, too." Though she was reason-ably sure he hadn't walked in her shoes.

"Soldiers get close. The band of brothers is real."

The conversation was getting heavy and Melody needed to lighten up. She brushed her bangs aside, fingertips skimming the scar. John North had scars, too.

"I saw your scars," she said, the image of his wide, buff chest and tapered waist teasing the edges of her memory. "Did you get wounded in combat?"

"A few times. No big deal."

"You really are a hero." The words were bitter on her tongue. She remembered another hero, a man she had loved with all her heart until he'd stolen everything and everyone that mattered. "Your family must be proud."

"I guess. Mostly, they want me to be safe and happy." His jaw softened as he spoke. She realized she'd been days with this man and hours on the phone but she knew little of his personal life.

"Do they live near here?"

"Mom and Dad do. Same ranch where I grew up just outside Glass Falls."

"Any brothers or sisters?" she asked, glad to ease the conversation toward the living and leave the dead alone.

"One sister in Wichita. I'm an uncle, too. Two nieces and a nephew. Real cute kids. Want to see pictures?"

He carried pictures of his sister's kids. Heartwarming.

"I'd love to."

He dug a stack of photos from his wallet and scooted his chair around so that they were side by side at the table. The scent of pine came with him, not unpleasant at all.

His shoulder brushed hers. She really should move away.

Chili whimpered and both of them looked in his direction. "A dream," John said.

"More likely a nightmare. He hates thunderstorms."

As if nature wanted to torture them all, a crash of thunder rattled the old building.

"This little man," John said, sliding a photo of a small, brown-haired boy under her nose, "is Kade. He's three. Funniest little dude you'll ever meet. Swims like a fish."

Melody expected to offer a polite comment and feel nothing, but the sweet, chubby-cheeked child touched an empty spot inside her. "He's adorable."

She didn't let herself think much about kids. She had her dogs. That was enough.

John showed her the other kids and then photos of his entire family, telling funny stories from childhood. Melody found herself laughing along with him.

John North was a pretty fun guy.

"How often do you get to see them?"

"Not often enough. I miss them a lot." He tilted back in his chair, hands locked behind his head. "Once I thought I'd have a few rug rats of my own, but—"

"You still can. You're not old."

He shook his head. "Nah. One divorce did it for me. I don't want to do that again."

Because she was every bit as cynical as he, Melody didn't say what was on her mind, that a man could marry and have kids without divorcing. To people like her and John, marriage meant divorce or worse. The worse was the part that kept her safely single.

"Well, the nieces and nephews are adorable," she said, proud of herself for shifting the conversation. "When they get bigger, you'll have to bring them to the mountains. Wichita is pretty flat, isn't it?"

He chuckled. "The flattest."

They talked then of mundane things, geography, the mountains, the troublesome rumors about the Emergency Management Department. Usually, she didn't get involved in other people or their problems, but John North was doing a good thing. People should leave him the heck alone.

After a long time, the shadows deepened and the fire burned low.

North got up to toss more wood in the fireplace. Sparks shot up. The scent of evergreen smoke curled into Melody's nostrils, pungent and warm.

"That's the last of the wood," John said, dusting his hands over his thighs. A thunderclap rattled the windows. "And it's still storming."

Mellowed by the last couple of hours of pleasant conversation, her response was more of a joke than a complaint. "We may be trapped here until we starve."

"Nah. We don't starve on my watch. A great hunter can bring home the bacon." He made a pistol with his fingers and pulled the invisible trigger.

The action sent trickles of anxiety racing over her nerve endings. "You don't have a gun."

"Could have fooled me. I thought this—" he reached into a jacket hanging over the back of his chair and pulled out a black pistol "—was called a gun."

The blood drained out of her head so fast, she felt dizzy. Her heart stopped, then started again, thundering like the storm outside.

He had a gun. They were alone…

And far, far from help.

CHAPTER SEVEN

"I DON'T LIKE GUNS."

John could see he'd made a mistake. Melody's face had gone as white as bleached socks, though the reaction surprised him. Tough and mountain smart, she knew the dangers out here. After years in the military and since sighting the cougar, he'd thought the addition of a weapon a logical decision. She clearly didn't agree.

"I'm an experienced marksman."

Her lips thinned into a grim line. "How reassuring."

"It's not loaded. See?" John slid the admittedly potent-looking clip from the pocket of soggy pants he'd hung over the rope. He held the clip out toward her. "Ammo's here. The gun's there."

She turned her head. "Great. Get it out of my sight."

John sighed. Maybe he'd been in the military too long. A weapon was as much a part of his attire as his boots. He stashed the weaponry back in their places.

"All gone now. You're safe."

Melody didn't say a word. She simply wrapped her lady-bug blanket around her shoulders and propped her back against the wall, staring off into a distant space that did not include him.

Disappointment settled in like morning fog. They'd been having a pleasant conversation, even laughing together. He was starting to know her better. And then bam! she clammed up again.

Melody had a habit of closing off to people, but he thought the two of them had spent enough time together to be friends. She should trust him by now.

"You gotta be tired," he said. "I know I am. We might as well get some rest."

Melody still didn't answer, and from her stony expression John figured she'd rather sleep out in the storm than in here with him. But she wasn't crazy, no matter what anybody said. She knew wet plus cold equaled hypothermia.

"This hut's going to get colder than a brass monkey when that fire burns down," he went on. "Why don't you stretch out closer to the fire?"

"You go ahead. I'm okay here." She stared at him one long moment and then closed her eyes to shut him out.

With a resigned shrug, John curled up in his green wool blanket next to the fire. The hard floor rubbed every protruding bone, but he'd slept on worse. As a Ranger, he'd learned to adjust to any environment rapidly, deal with it and survive.

He could hear Melody breathing and knew she wasn't asleep. The last few minutes replayed in his mind. He'd upset her with the mere mention of a gun. Lots of people disliked arms, but Melody's reaction seemed deeper somehow.

Another missing piece in the Melody Crawford puzzle.

A spark crackled in the fireplace. The dog shifted, then

settled again. In the far corner, the leaky roof drip-dripped onto the wood floor.

Melody Crawford. She had a wall around her thicker than the mountains. Today she'd been gruff at times and short-spoken as though he'd done something to tick her off. Yet when he'd teased her, she'd returned as good as he gave. She was strong and independent, but tonight he'd glanced behind the curtain, seen her witty, softer side. From the first moment he'd laid eyes on her, he'd been interested, but now he thought he actually liked the woman. Or he had until she'd shut him out.

When she'd changed clothes, he'd been sorely tempted to peek, though the gentleman in him had resisted. As cute as she was in jeans and flannel shirt, she'd be killer sexy in lace underwear. He knew she wore them. Pink ones. He'd glimpsed a pair when she'd dumped her backpack.

His body reacted to the fantasy. Not good. Not good at all. He refocused, concentrating on the way she'd raced to his aid today when a tree limb had slapped his face and knocked him backward on his behind.

Her hands had been all over him, checking for injuries. He'd liked that. He'd even considered hurting himself in some other way just to get her to touch him.

He grinned into the darkness.

She'd been all gentle concern. When the alcohol wipe against his cheek had made his eyes water, she'd called him a wimp, but she'd sympathized, too, by blowing on the offended scratch. Her lips had been so close to his, he'd been tempted to kiss her.

He, who'd sworn off women, wanted to kiss a porcupine.

With those amused thoughts, he dozed.

Sometime later, he awoke to a darkened room, lit only by

the faintest glow of embers. The room was cold. Not nearly as cold as outdoors, he thought, but too cold for comfort.

At some point the storm had subsided, though a howling wind rattled the window and crawled beneath the door like icy, reaching fingers. No wonder he felt chilled.

He pressed the tiny illumination stem on his watch. Three o'clock glowed eerie green. A few more hours until daylight.

He rolled to his other side, concerned about Melody. There she was, still sitting against the wall, her head lolled to one side in miserable slumber. She was too far from the fireplace, which wasn't much, but any heat source was better than the cold, damp wall. Stubborn woman.

She shifted, murmuring softly, then tried to burrow deeper into the ladybug blanket. The cute, girlish blanket had surprised him as much as the lacy underwear. For a woman who was no-nonsense to a fault, the whimsical discrepancy was revealing.

She'd already been sexy to him, but now that he'd witnessed this feminine side of her, he couldn't get her out of his head. Or maybe it was the situation. Stranded alone in a tiny cabin with no one around for miles.

She moved again, shivered. One sock-covered foot poked out from her small blanket. He wished he'd had something warmer for her to sleep in.

With a sigh, he sat up and watched her for a moment, thinking. Would she appreciate his interference? Or kick him in the teeth?

He'd been raised to protect and provide for the female gender, no matter how strong they were. Call it testosterone, call it chauvinistic, he didn't care. To him, the reaction was genetically ingrained in the male animal. If a woman was in need, he was expected to take care of the problem. End of subject. Especially since he wondered if Melody Crawford was really as tough as she let on.

There was something especially fragile about her in sleep. In the shadowy fire glow, she appeared young and helpless, her full upper lip pouty and soft-looking. Kissable. Real kissable.

But he was not the kind of man to take advantage.

With a sigh, John moved silently to her side. He stood, studying her. Finally, he slid down next to her, supported her shoulders and head, and gently eased her lax body to the floor.

He held his breath, waiting for her to awaken and punch his lights out. When she didn't, he gingerly stretched beside her for warmth. That was all, just warmth. He was a survivalist. So was she.

Melody made a noise, a cross between a murmur and a moan, and scooted closer. Her nose bumped his hand. She was as cold as frozen cod. Practicality said for him to put his arms around her. He eased one arm up, let it hover above her while his heart did weird things inside his chest.

He was a Ranger, a man who could block out the physical and emotional and do what needed to be done. The mission was everything. And the mission was staying warm until morning.

With gritted teeth, he gently wrapped his arms around her and brought her close to his chest. She burrowed in like a little bunny rabbit seeking a fluffy nest.

John's pulse skittered, danced and finally set up a steady jackhammer.

They were thigh to thigh, chest to chest, his arms cradling her close like a child. But she was not a child.

Melody Crawford felt sweet and soft and sexy in his arms. Curved in all the right places, she was completely female and more tempting than he'd imagined. And yes, he had imagined.

Even her scent, a mixture of the forest and her own subtly fragrant skin, taunted him.

He bit down on the inside of his cheek and envisioned jumping into a frozen stream. Naked.

No, not naked. He didn't want to think about naked bodies.

She stirred again and John stilled. Her wiggles did ferocious things to him. One of her hands snaked between them and came to rest against his neck. Her fingers flexed, stroking the shock of hair behind his ear. Tickling. Torturing.

He swallowed a groan.

Morning couldn't get here soon enough.

Melody awakened slowly from the pleasant dream. She was toasty warm and feeling mellow, almost happy. What had she dreamed?

Her right hand seemed paralyzed, trapped somehow. She tried to move it and couldn't. Something heavy held it fast. She was also sandwiched between two warm sources. The dogs?

Slowly, awareness grew. No, not the dogs. Although she suspected Chili was lying behind her, the other body was decidedly male. Human male. Her stomach quivered. A very strong arm circled her back and rested on her shoulder, fingers trailing so near her breasts they tingled. Another hand had taken up residence on her bottom in a most possessive fashion.

She was wrapped in John North's embrace.

Her heart thumped once, hard, suddenly remembering her dream. A dream of John North…and her.

How had this happened? When had she snuggled close—enticingly close—to John?

Though they were lying on a hard floor in a musty-smelling cabin, she didn't want to move. She felt secure. Safe even.

How crazy was that?

She listened. The storm had stopped, but the wind howled like a hundred coyotes. Behind her Chili snored. In front of her, John's chest rose and fell against hers in a steady rhythm. He was asleep.

She slowly peeked beneath her lashes, loath to spoil this strangely restful moment. The first gray light of morning crept through the dirty window.

North still hadn't moved, so Melody opened her eyes all the way. She shouldn't have.

Even bathed in peaceful sleep, John North was a warrior, ready for battle, strong and proud and self-confident. A ruggedly beautiful male, far too masculine to be pretty but too manly to be ignored.

His hair was disheveled, enticingly messy, so that she longed to smooth it down and let her fingers play there. The night's beard outlined his mouth in sexy relief. There was tenderness there, too, in the curve and shape of his lips. She wondered what kissing him would be like.

The idea jolted her sense of reserve. She never thought about a man this way, not since the nightmare that took everything. What was the matter with her this morning?

She'd never been lonely. Alone yes, but not lonely. She preferred being alone. She had her dogs. She was busy, useful, the best search and rescue trainer around.

She neither needed nor wanted a man in her life.

He opened his eyes and the thoughts faltered.

Sleepy, heavy-lidded eyes trapped hers. His mouth curved. "'Morning."

His husky rumble vibrated from his chest to hers. She was afraid to move, lest he realize how closely pressed they were.

"Hi." The whisper responded to the trembling in her belly. "Sleep well?"

As hard as she tried, Melody couldn't take her eyes off his mouth.

"Like a rock." The words were softly murmured, intimate, not like her at all. "You?"

His gaze dropped to her mouth. His tone, too, was low, sexy, suggesting things. Things she wanted to hear. "Better than I expected after we joined forces. You snuggle real good."

The heat of a blush warmed her cheeks. Apparently, she'd sought him out sometime during the cold night. Unbelievable.

"Can you blame me?" she murmured, in one last-ditch effort to maintain control. "You're warm." And hard. But she didn't mention that.

"Mmm. You're soft as a kitten." The hand that grazed her breast moved to her cheek. His voice dropped to a whisper. "So soft. Drives a man crazy."

Melody swallowed. What she saw in John's eyes melted her bones. Like two powerful magnets they moved closer. John stroked her cheek, let his fingers graze the corner of her mouth, the rough, calloused thumb a seduction against her sensitive skin. She shivered, her lips parting. His strong hand guided her closer.

She placed a palm on his chest, felt the hammer of his heart. A warrior's heart that beat for her.

And that was Melody's undoing.

In the next instant, John's mouth possessed hers in sweet and gentle persuasion. Bolts of electricity far more powerful than last night's storm ricocheted from his lips to her brain and throughout her body. The world outside faded. She forgot time, forgot place, forgot everything but the pleasure of being in John's arms, of sharing this morning kiss.

She was lost and yet, she was home.

Her arms snaked up around his neck. She stroked the coarse thickness of hair, pressing ever closer.

John's tender-rough hands cupped her face. He made a noise in the back of his throat, half growl, half groan. Melody felt both powerful and powerless as John North ignited feelings long sublimated.

Last night, she'd worried about the pistol, but this morning she recognized the truth. The greatest danger from John North was not to her person, but to her heart.

With regret, she did what had to be done and slowly broke away from the world-changing kiss.

John reached for her. "More," he whispered.

That single word nearly shattered her, but she fought against the unwanted feelings and broke away. She leaped to her feet, afraid if she didn't get as far away as possible, she would succumb to the sweet temptation. She would become vulnerable. And vulnerability could get you killed.

She couldn't risk being close ever again, even when it felt so right. Trusting brought pain. Melody Crawford had long ago surrendered the childhood fantasy that a handsome white knight would keep her safe from evil. The evil had gotten there first.

John rolled up on one elbow to watch Melody fidget around the tiny room, her movements jerky as she sorted their meager breakfast rations. No matter how hard he stared, she refused to look at him.

His body still throbbed with longing to hold her. Something else throbbed, too—his heart. Melody was getting to him.

She'd kissed him with enough passion to melt steel and then shoved him away so fast his blood still thundered through his veins. And now she wouldn't look at him. He was pretty sure she wouldn't talk to him, either. She was like a spooked deer, all big, soft eyes and skittish movements.

The first question was why? The second bothered him even more. Why did he care one way or the other?

With an inward groan, he pushed away his blanket and headed outside. A few minutes in the cold would clear his head and cool his blood. Right now, he was confused and a tad bit annoyed. And he didn't have time for such emotional turmoil. He had a department to build, not much time to build it and failure was not an option.

"Come on, Chili," he said, using the dog as an excuse to break the painful silence. "Time to find a bush."

Melody waited until the door closed to glance in that direction. John North was angry. An angry man was dangerous. Seeing her chance, she quickly went to the bag where he'd stashed the pistol and removed it. No need to look around the room to know there was no place to hide the weapon, so she slipped it into her backpack. Somewhere along the trek back to the truck, she'd toss the horrid thing off a cliff.

With a relieved exhale, she got dressed for the journey home, finding her coat and gloves damp on the outside but dry inside.

Footsteps sounded on the porch. The door opened. The wind blew John and a prancing Chili into the room.

"Brr," John said. "Cold." In the few minutes outside, the wind had whipped color into his cheeks.

Their eyes met. Melody had a flashback of how warm and

solid he was, and of how cozy she'd felt in his arms. Nothing about him appeared dangerous.

But there were questions in his eyes and a gentle accusation that left her guilt-ridden. He didn't understand why she'd responded to his kiss with such longing and then bolted like a madwoman.

And she couldn't even begin to explain.

Hiding the pistol had been foolish, a knee-jerk reaction to the past. John North would not harm her. At least not with a gun.

At a loss, she spun to the table for Chili's breakfast. Unprepared for an overnight stay all she could offer was a pack of snacks, the jerky John had brought along for her dogs. Had she thanked him for that?

Chili took the treats in quick gulps. He'd expended a lot of energy yesterday without much fuel. On one knee, she ruffled his fur and hugged him. He served as a much-needed buffer between her and John North.

Her stomach rumbled.

"Better eat something," John said, reaching around her for the peanut butter and crackers. "I looked for some dry wood to restart the fire but everything is soaked. A real breakfast and hot coffee will have to wait."

The mention of food and survival, the common everyday tasks of her life eased the knot in her belly.

"Coffee," she groaned, resigning herself to trail mix and the final bottle of water. "Do you know how good that sounds?"

"Not as good as pancakes."

"Oh, please. Do not say pancakes."

His eyes crinkled. "Hot, fluffy pancakes dripping with butter and syrup."

Melody groaned and closed her eyes.

"And a side of crispy fried bacon," John added, then snitched a handful of her trail mix and went to the window.

Melody swigged the water and stared at his backside, unable to clear her head of that moment in his arms. She'd been as much to blame as him, maybe more so. But he'd messed with her mind, what was left of it, and the poor man didn't have a clue.

Or maybe he did. A man like North wasn't a stranger to women.

After a bit, while they both crunched peanuts, John shifted. Melody, afraid he'd catch her staring, studied the toes of her boots. She needed a new pair, but with Ace's surgery, boots would have to wait.

"Come here," John said, turning slightly. "I want to show you something."

Melody hesitated. Then because she felt guilty about the kiss and for taking the gun, she did as he asked.

"Look at that," he murmured, his voice reverent as he pointed toward the east.

The window was narrow and for them both to look out required a closeness that buzzed through her like some high-energy drink. But she didn't want to cause another rift by moving away. Most likely, North already questioned the wisdom of taking her on as an employee. And she needed this job. Sometimes, her memories crowded out her common sense.

Her shoulder grazed his, and he shifted again, making room for her at the window.

Morning had broken over a jagged, snowcapped mountain, the sun a coral fire behind it. Clouds swirled around the mountain peak, occasionally dipping to weave like ghostly images through the spruce and fir. And over all of this drifted snowflakes the size of silver dollars.

"Beautiful," she said. A lump formed beneath her breast-bone. She would never get enough of the stunning, unexpected gifts of the mountains.

His finger touched the window. "See the ptarmigan?"

She squinted through the dirty pane, knowing the white bird could easily be camouflaged by the snow. "Ah, there she is."

"Or he. Probably looking for his mate. Did you know ptarmigan mate for life but spend the winter apart?"

"How do they find each other again in spring?"

"No one knows for sure. Instinct, I guess. My sister used to say their hearts call to each other."

Melody tilted her head to look at him, moved by the lovely sentiment. "What a nice thought."

He glanced down, gaze sincere as he touched her cheek. "Are we okay?"

She didn't pretend not to understand.

"Sure," she said. As okay as they'd ever be.

"I hope I didn't cross some invisible line."

Melody stepped back, breaking contact. She couldn't look at him and lie. "We shared a meaningless kiss, North. No big deal. Forget about it."

She would try her best to take her own advice, but there was nothing meaningless in the way he'd held and kissed her, nor in the way she'd responded like a starved-for-affection old maid.

After a beat of silence, North turned his attention to the scene outside. Melody struggled with the need to say more, to clarify, but no words came. She vacillated between self-preservation and bitter regret. He'd kissed her. She'd kissed him back. She'd liked it. Too much. How could she blame him for that?

John's jaw worked, but his face was otherwise impassive.

Whatever was going on behind those brown eyes would remain a secret.

"Time to break camp," he said.

And time to break away from the need to explain, to get out of here before she did something stupid again.

CHAPTER EIGHT

THEY MADE THE TRIP back to the trailhead in rapid silence, talking only when the need arose. The dark red dog raced ahead as if understanding the importance of getting back to civilization or at least to communication. Melody may not need the outside world, but John did. He'd been out of contact with the dispatcher for hours now. If any problems had arisen in his absence, he was screwed.

Halfway down, Melody paused to point out an elk hidden in the trees. Another time, she took his offered hand as they churned up a particularly steep incline. Moments like that convinced John that she bore him no ill will, maybe even liked him. But they puzzled him, too.

Regardless of her denial, he'd crossed a line by kissing her. Trouble was, if he had to relive the moment, he'd do the same thing all over again. One kiss had only whetted his appetite and affirmed his belief that Melody was a pretty special lady underneath those quills.

He smiled to himself as his truck jounced over low water crossings and started the climb to her place. The two-mile driveway was about as primitive as a road could get.

Holding hard to the jostling wheel, he glanced at his rider.

"I couldn't beg a cup of coffee from you while I make some calls, could I?"

"Only a wretch would deny a person coffee."

He pulled into her yard, noticed the snow was thicker here. "You got snow instead of rain last night. Soft powder. The skiers would love it."

She slammed out of the truck and unloaded Chili without answering. "I have to see about my dogs first."

"I'll check on the dogs if you'll make coffee."

The ghost of a smile lit her eyes. "Works for me."

Leaving a trail of footprints in the pristine snow, she marched into the house.

The dogs looked fine to him, but John replaced their frozen water with fresh before tromping to the house. At the back door, he stomped his feet, freeing them from snow and also to warn Melody of his arrival. He'd been in her house before to less than a warm welcome.

She appeared, pushed the door open and offered him a steaming cup.

He almost fell at her feet in worship. "Awesome."

After one scalding sip, John set the cup aside to cool while he fished out his telephone. He frowned at the now activated screen. "I've got ten messages."

All last night, the phone had been dead and someone had been trying to reach him. A foreboding spoiled the pleasure of hot coffee and a warm house.

When he listened to the urgent messages, the foreboding grew. He punched in a number, and as he spoke briefly he went as cold as his toes. "What happened?"

Melody came padding in from the back room with the German shepherd. The dog moved stiffly but didn't seem in pain. That was a big improvement. John trailed his free hand across the noble head, his real focus on the troubling conversation.

"Where?"

Melody caught the anxiety in his tone and came to stand in front of him, head tilted in question.

"What is it?" she mouthed.

He shook his head and held up a hand.

"Be there in ten minutes." He snapped the phone shut.

"Trouble?"

"The worst. A plane went down last night in the storm."

"Oh, no." Neither had to voice what this meant. He was the director of the department. This was his responsibility and he hadn't been there.

He apprised her of as much information as he knew. "I'm out of here. You coming?"

She pushed a toaster pastry into his hand. "Go. Chili needs a good meal first. I'll be there soon."

He was out the door and halfway to the truck before she finished.

The command center was already set up and in full swing when John arrived at the Volunteer Fire Station. A beehive of activity buzzed around the small facility as volunteers gathered. Law enforcement, forestry workers, paramedics and everyday people who knew the mountains had come to offer help. The only people John wasn't glad to see were the reporters.

Blood rushing in his temples, he surveyed the crowded room, listening to the hum of conversation and finally homed in on the county sheriff, Brent Page. A harried Brent gnawed a half-disintegrated cigarette as if his life depended on it.

"Sheriff," John said, dispensing with a greeting. "Apprise me of the situation, will you?"

He hated starting out behind. The last time he'd been in that situation, one of his unit had gone down.

"North! Gol dang, man. Where you been? I tried half the night to reach you." Page gnawed the cigarette in agitation. "All hell's broke loose."

He was afraid of that.

"Got caught in the thunderstorm." Not an excuse, but a reason.

"Yeah, well, so did an Albuquerque lawyer and his two sons." The cancer stick bobbed up and down. "Bad deal. Real bad deal. Weather up there's tricky. I hope you've got some magic up your sleeve that I don't know about."

The grim reality struck North like a blow. He hadn't been here. If casualties were taken, they were his failure. Maybe he should have braved the storm last night instead of making camp, but it was too late to consider that now.

"Who called in the emergency personnel?"

"I put Deputy Clausen on that fancy address book of yours. He took care of it."

John gave a short nod, thankful he'd spent the time putting the hodgepodge of contact numbers into one easily accessed file. "I owe him one."

And he meant that. Time was crucial, though bad weather could hold search efforts at bay for hours, days even.

Tad chose that moment to breeze in, looking fresh as a daisy. John would bet a bundle Clausen had had his coffee this morning. Lucky sucker.

"Well, lookie here," Tad said, slowly removing his aviator sunglasses, "at who decided to show up this morning. And looking a little rough around the edges, too. Bad night? Or maybe a real good one?"

In another situation, North would enjoy wiping the smirk from Tad's face, but today people's lives were at stake.

Swallowing his pride, he said, "Thanks for calling in the volunteers."

"Somebody had to do it. You were…indisposed. I couldn't get hold of that spooky dog woman, either." Tad's eyes glinted with glee. "Wonder why that was? Were you keeping her busy with other duties last night?"

John clenched his back teeth. He was too tired for this. And he hadn't had his coffee. Tad had no idea the danger he was in.

With rigid control, John refrained from tearing Tad's throat out. Insulting him was one thing. Insulting the lady just wouldn't cut it.

"If you have a problem with me, Deputy, we'll settle it. But not here and not now. And consider this a warning, keep your mouth shut about Miss Crawford. We've got a job to do this morning. Let's get to it."

Tad puffed up like an adder, longing to strike but not quite sure he could handle the fury radiating from his adversary. Animosity crackled in the air like static electricity.

John held the glare until Tad backed down and shoved his sunglasses into place. "Just a joke, man. Come on. Don't be so touchy."

Right, Tad was joking. And John was Tinker Bell.

Twitching his shoulders to release the tension, John switched gears. "I meant it, Clausen. I appreciate your help." He hoped the man was mollified enough to back off. "Now, give me the rundown. Last sighting. Everything we know. Everything that's been done."

A flush crested the deputy's cheekbones and he was none too cordial, but he ticked off the information with rapid-fire efficiency. Brent Page added bits and pieces, including a conversation with the air traffic control out of Albuquerque.

John turned to the bulletin board to post a large map. He poked a red pushpin into the New Mexico city and another into the general area above Tabor Pass. The pilot had filed a flight plan and the last radar ping was somewhere over this remote, rugged region at the top of the world. So far, no transponder signal was forthcoming from the downed plane. And that was not a good sign.

"Do we have a chopper available?" An air search was their best bet, if the weather cooperated.

"Already on the way," Tad answered, ready to gloat again. "I know how to run an operation like this."

"Good. We need all the help we can get." John shoved a satellite photo of Tabor Pass into Tad's hands. The area was far away from any place he and Melody had explored, so they'd have to go with whatever topographical information they could find. "Make copies of this for the searchers while I break them into teams and make assignments. If air support spots anything, searchers on the ground can be ready to roll."

Tad's nostrils flared. He snatched the photo from John's hand, pivoted and disappeared. Over the next thirty minutes, John was too busy to breathe, much less to worry about Tad's bad attitude.

He longed for a cup of coffee and a real breakfast but his needs would have to wait. As tired as he was after the miserable night, the passengers in that plane needed help now—if any had survived.

An hour later, when a black-haired woman with a red dog

entered the fire station, John's heart leaped. No time to examine the emotion, other than to acknowledge that she and the dog added another dimension to the search possibilities. They may not be able to go up in the chopper but they were here if needed, and Melody knew this entire region as well as anyone.

Striding into the command post with more determination than energy, she looked every bit as tired as he. One glance at John and she headed straight for the coffeepot.

"Here," she said, pushing the disposable cup into his hands. "You look like you could use this."

"I've been too busy to bother. Thanks." He gazed at Melody over the rim as he sipped, inappropriately happy to see her, considering they'd been together for more than twenty-four hours straight.

"Sit down before you fall down," she said, pulling a chair toward him.

"Can't. Gotta make more calls."

"Do you have an assignment for Chili and me?"

"Not yet. The plane apparently went down over Tabor Pass. The place is impossible to reach by land in a timely manner. If the search chopper makes a positive sighting, I've got another chopper waiting to take up rescue teams."

"Can someone take us up to the Pass now? Or get us close? If there are survivors they may try to walk out. Chili can find them before they get too far away from the crash site to be rescued."

He knew that. He also knew injured parties got disoriented and wandered away from the scene. He'd seen it in the military.

"Hey, John," someone hollered over the drone of ringing phones and the buzz of conversations.

John spun toward the dispatcher. "Yes, ma'am? Got anything?"

"The chopper's having problems. They're setting down at a ranch until the weather eases up."

That was news John did not want to hear, though he wasn't surprised. He'd talked to the National Weather Service himself.

"We're going to have to try something else," Melody said, worrying her bottom lip.

With a fleeting flashback of tasting that lip, John said, "Yes. But what?"

They had every available resource on alert, but no one could move. His special ops training clicked through his head in a rapid slide show of options considered and discarded until a new idea took root. Rangers worked with whatever the mission gave them. They problem-solved on the move, improvising, finding new solutions to old problems. Sometimes a man needed a little help from his friends.

"Georgia," he said to the dispatcher. "Get Kirtland Air Force Base on the line. Ask for Colonel Grimes."

The air force had the Osprey, a hybrid plane-chopper that could fly and land where choppers couldn't, and Kirkland was not far away. If the Osprey was available to assist, the lawyer and his sons' chances for survival went up a notch.

"Do you have an idea?" Melody asked.

"Yes, ma'am, I do. Let's see if the boys in blue want to come out and play with their fancy toys." Adrenaline pumping, he gave her a wink and strode across the room to the dispatch cubicle.

While he waded through the military protocol at Kirtland, he watched Melody, a small island unto herself. She'd sat down at an empty table, her chin resting on the heel of her hand, a map spread on the table before her. Chili made the rounds of the room, schmoozing enough for both of them. She sat back, rolled her shoulders, then shot a hand through her hair. She was restless, either eager to get to work or eager to escape the crowded room. Probably both.

She took a pencil from somewhere and scribbled furiously on the map.

Just as Colonel Grimes came on the line, she took a sip of his coffee. John's belly tightened at the personal, almost intimate gesture. He turned his back away from the distraction.

In minutes, he hung up the phone, renewed energy surging through his veins like caffeine. Returning his attention to Melody, he found her watching him, expression hopeful. At his thumbs-up, she smiled. Eager to share the news, he wove his way through the huddle of people bunched around a box of doughnuts.

Before he could reach her, Tad Clausen sauntered up to the table, thumbs hooked in his belt buckle. Melody flushed deep red at something the deputy said. She shook her head and stared down. Tad placed both hands on the table and leaned toward her.

John increased his pace, politely shrugging off a woman with a tape recorder. Tad's back was turned to him, but John had a clear vision of Melody's distressed face.

When he drew close enough, he stopped, staying out of Tad's sight long enough to hear what was being said.

"Leave me alone, Tad."

"Not until you tell me about last night." The deputy's voice was quietly vicious. "Where were you and North? I know you were together. Both of you look like something the cat dug up."

Gaze defiant, Melody told the truth. "We got caught in the thunderstorm."

"Come on, honey. This is old Tad you're talking to." He leaned in with a stage whisper. "What were the two of you doing up there all night? Things you wouldn't do with me?"

John had heard enough. He grabbed Tad's shoulder. "I warned you, Clausen. Back off."

The deputy shrugged his hand away. "What's the matter, North? Afraid I'll cut in on your action?"

John counted to three and then thought, screw it. The guy needs a pounding. He grabbed Tad's shirt and yanked him close. A slight twist and he cut off the man's air supply.

"Shut your filthy mouth," he murmured in a low, furious tone. "Not another word. Hear me?"

Tad's eyes bulged. He struggled helplessly.

Melody put a hand on John's arm. "John, please. Don't make a scene. The search."

She was right. This wasn't the time or place. Shaking off the boiling fury, he released the deputy.

Red faced and trembling with rage, Tad swiped at the spittle gathered at the corner of his mouth. His nostrils flared. "You're gonna pay for that, North. You and your little witch."

Then he spun away on his boot heel and stalked outside toward the news media gathered in the parking lot.

John watched him go, dismay and dread in his gut.

"If he says one negative word to the media…"

"He's more interested in getting his picture on TV."

"I hope you're right, but I doubt it."

He shouldn't have lost his cool. In fact, John couldn't believe he'd snapped like that. He, a man renowned for cool under pressure, had snapped like a twig. This was not a good sign.

He glanced down at a distressed Melody.

"Are you okay?" he asked.

She nodded, though her hands fisted at her side and her eyes were overbright. "Forget about it, North. I can handle Tad."

It hit him then. "This isn't the first time he's hassled you, is it?"

She looked away. "Tad's always been a jerk."

He touched her shoulder. "Hey, talk to me."

She shook away the command. "He's not worth the breath it takes."

Gently, John turned her around. "If he ever bothers you again, I want to know about it."

Her chin went up. "I can take care of myself."

He wanted to kiss that stubborn mouth. "Not on my watch."

When her bulldog expression didn't falter, he let his gaze slide around the room and then come back to her. Dark half moons formed inverted crescents beneath her eyes.

"You're tired. Go home."

"I want to find that plane."

"So do I." He told her about the Osprey. "Until we hear from the air force or the chopper already up there, all we can do is wait. You might as well get some rest so you're fresh if we need you."

Weariness had settled into Melody's bones like a bad case of the flu. "Will you call me?"

"If a ground search becomes necessary."

"Fair enough." She gazed at the lines of fatigue around John's mouth, worrying. He was every bit as weary as she. Immediately, she scoffed at the concern. He was a former Ranger. Rangers could go days without rest.

She called Chili to heel and left the station. Two blocks

down, she wheeled into Chet's Diner, ordered a to-go break-fast and took it back to the command post.

"Hey, North." She slapped the container onto a folding table. John, in quiet conversation with a man in insulated coveralls, looked up.

"Thought you were gone."

"I am." She pushed the box at him. "Eat."

Whipping around, she left again, but not before she saw the shocked grin on North's face.

CHAPTER NINE

MELODY AWAKENED hours later. Other than a dull headache, she felt a lot better. Though she didn't want to care, she couldn't help wondering about North. By now, he must be dead on his feet. She wondered, too, if they'd found the plane or had any news at all.

After checking her messages and finding none, she thought about calling, but changed her mind. He said he'd call if she was needed. Right now, she had work to do here.

Ace's exercises had been neglected so she started with him, carefully massaging the weak muscles and then putting him through the paces to gain strength and flexibility. Such a trouper, he did everything she asked of him.

Afterward, she worked each of her student dogs through a training session, leaving Chili to rest in case he was called upon to search. The descending temperatures served as a constant reminder of the downed plane, of people up there in the mountains helpless and frightened and probably hurt.

She understood their horror and wished she and Chili could get busy. She wanted to find them.

Back in the house, she checked the messages again.

Nothing. Itching to know what was happening she lifted the receiver and then put it down again. John said he would call.

The sun set. Melody ate a bowl of chicken noodle soup, added a few pieces to a five-thousand-piece jigsaw puzzle, and finally curled up in a chair to sew some blocks for a quilt she was donating to a battered women's shelter.

Her feet grew cold. As she wrapped them in a brightly flowered fleece blanket, her thoughts slid to last night in the cold cabin with John. She shouldn't have let him kiss her. But the memory of that moment lingered like the fragrance of roses.

Getting their relationship back on a cool, professional level was not going to be easy.

She thought about quitting her job. One look at the German shepherd curled beside the furnace put an end to that kind of thinking.

She jabbed a needle into a pincushion and pushed the pile of cloth off her lap, getting up. Chili raised his head, a question in his eyes. She had the same question. What was going on down at the command center? With night coming on, if the plane crash victims hadn't been found, the odds were against survival.

North should have called by now. He should have updated her. Lifting the telephone receiver, she punched in his number, ready to give him a piece of her mind.

"North." He sounded so weary, she softened.

"How were the pancakes?"

"Delicious." She heard the smile in his voice. "I was about to call you."

Right. "Has the plane been located?"

"Yes. Not in Tabor Pass as radar indicated, but farther down the mountain. The great news is, we have survivors."

"That's terrific, John. Congratulations."

"Don't congratulate me yet." The weariness again. "The sons were airlifted out to Boulder with serious injuries. The pilot is missing."

"Oh, no."

"By all indications, he decided to walk out for help."

"What's the plan? Should we try to go up tonight?"

"We've called off the search until morning, Mel."

"I'll go now. Tell me where and get me up there. My dogs work anytime, day or night."

"Not a chance. The dark is not the biggest issue and you know it. It's the dark coupled with the elements. Right now, the area is covered in fog. Trust me, if I thought we could do this safely, we'd be up there."

Interesting that he'd said we. But she knew he was right about the search effort. Daylight would be safer and more productive, but she didn't like the delay. A man was lost in the bitter night and her dog could find him.

Frustration made her short. "What time then?"

"Four. I want to be on the ground at daybreak."

She blew out an annoyed sigh. "Fine."

The line hummed with silence. She should hang up. The conversation was over.

"Melody?"

"Yes?"

A pause and then, "See you in the morning."

The simple phrase held a wealth of meaning in Melody's troubled mind. Anticipation, not only for the search and rescue ahead but to see him again, coursed through her veins. She didn't want to feel the things John North was forcing her to feel.

She replaced the telephone receiver and went to the cheval mirror where she pushed her jagged bangs away from her forehead, holding them back with one hand while she leaned in and traced the white scar with one finger. Here was the only reason she needed, the only reminder required.

A war raged in her mind. John North had been good and kind to her, but so had the murderer. John had kissed her, holding her as if she were fragile and special. But trust would get her hurt.

Chili padded into the room and sat on his rump, watching her. She dropped a hand to his perked ears. A heavy sadness settled into her chest.

She had her dogs. That's all she could ever have.

Tomorrow she must face John North with a cold, set heart. Tomorrow she must not forget.

The helicopter ride was exhilarating, the scenery breathtaking, and yet the tension inside the noisy chopper was thicker than pea soup.

John didn't know what was going on inside Melody's head but she was quiet and withdrawn this morning. He could relate, in a way. He'd slept little last night thinking of the morning's chore. But something more was troubling Melody. Sometimes he wished she'd open up and talk to him, and the thought amused him. He, a man not given to needless chatter, wanted a woman to tell him things.

During his hours of tossing and turning, trying to figure out the best way to save the lost pilot, Melody had invaded his mind. She had secrets, something so painful she'd withdrawn from people. Any fool could figure that out. But John wanted to know what to do about it. The bigger question was why he cared in the first place, but he'd finally come to grips with that last night, too.

Melody got to him on some elemental level. He wouldn't go as far as love, but he felt something for her.

Responsibility, maybe. Yeah, he felt responsible for her, protective as he had been with his Ranger unit. That was it. That had to be it.

The whump-whump of the helicopter grew louder as they descended onto the side of mountain. Snow blew up in every direction clouding the view below, but John knew the drill. Last night's chopper pilot had made base at a remote ranch a thousand feet down from the crash site. They would start the search at the ranch and hike upward to the scene. Considering the rugged, almost impossible terrain, this plan was the best they could do.

By daylight the entire group of searchers had hiked to the crash site. A cold sun broke over the mountain as four search and rescue teams and their animals started off in different directions, breaths puffing smoke signals into the atmosphere, each pair armed with a crackling radio and backpacks of needed supplies.

John fell in step beside Melody and received a scowl for his efforts. "Forget it, North."

"You heard the briefing. Everyone works in pairs. The terrain is too dangerous to be alone."

"My dog and I are a pair." She tromped off without him, but he kept pace. Snow spun up around them like powdered sugar in a mixing bowl.

"The dog doesn't count," John said, staying right in step.

She whipped toward him, teeth gritted. "Then get me someone else."

John stepped back, speechless. Melody didn't mind working in a team, but she didn't want him. He rubbed a hand down the silky front of his parka, over his heart. Her rejection hurt more than it should have.

"Who peed in your porridge?"

Melody's mouth twitched. Good. He was getting somewhere. "You have a way with words, North."

"Well?" he demanded. She had no reason to show her quills this morning unless... "Still mad because I kissed you?"

Again, she stopped in the trail, silvery-gold eyes snapping. "Please go back to base. Now."

Ah, so it *was* the kiss. The revelation actually made him feel better. The fact that she was still upset about the kiss must mean she cared one way or the other. He wasn't sure why that encouraged him, but it did.

"You're stuck with me, Crawford. Deal with it."

Melody emitted a beleaguered huff. "Then shut up and move. We have a man to find."

She was right about that, but he was right about something else. She was his responsibility and she was not going this one alone, regardless of any sputtering she might do. John could handle her blustering. Another team member might not understand.

Right. As if he did.

One thing he did know: her bark was far worse than her bite. Only a deeply caring woman would be up here on this frigid, dangerous mountain trying to find a total stranger. Besides, she liked him enough to buy him breakfast. He smiled to himself. Yep. Melody could bark all she wanted. But he suspected the noise was only a smoke screen.

She bent to unsnap Chili's leash, standing quietly while the dog acclimated himself to the sights, sounds and smells. Chili's coat shone like a copper penny in the startling sunlight as he wiggled in excitement for the search ahead. Melody spoke a short, gentle command and the amazing canine darted off, nostrils popping as he searched the invisible scent particles.

The humans proceeded along behind him with much more care for the terrain. This high up the opportunities to fall into a crevice or off a snow-laden cliff rose exponentially. And avalanche was always a deadly possibility.

John lifted his binoculars, hoping to spot any flash of light or color against the backdrop of white snow and deep gray rock. Melody occasionally paused to call out the pilot's name and blow a whistle. "Jeff!"

The pillows of snow absorbed the sound at once and no answering call came. After an hour or so, they took a short break. Melody checked the dog's paws and carefully cleaned his snout, then fed him an energy snack.

"I don't think the pilot came this way," Melody said.

John handed her a granola bar. "Why not?"

She shrugged, peeling back the wrapper. "A gut feeling."

As a Ranger, he respected instinct. Many a man had been saved by listening to that inner voice.

"What do you suggest?"

"You're the man in charge. I'm working my sector as ordered." Watching him, she bit down on the end of the snack. He could swear she was teasing.

He grinned. "Crawford, you're something."

One dark eyebrow arched in agreement, she tilted her head. The hint of amusement danced behind those mysterious eyes. John fought a sharp, annoyingly inappropriate desire to grab her and kiss her right then and there.

Being with Melody was causing him to lose his edge, his focus. A man's life was in jeopardy and all he could think about was kissing the dog trainer. She was right. He should have paired her with someone else.

With the steely discipline of his training, he shut off all thoughts of the woman beside him to radio base and each of the dog teams to determine progress. With no news, he said to Melody, "Let's go ahead and finish this sector so we can mark the area off the map."

"Okay." She unsnapped the Lab again and spoke the command, sending Chili back to work.

As time passed, John's face grew numb and even behind the sunglasses his eyes burned from the cold wind, but he ignored them, focusing instead on the unstable terrain. In another couple of months, some of the snow would be gone and searching would be easier, but accidents didn't wait for summer. If the plane's pilot was not cognitively impaired, a real concern, he would work his way downhill. If he was hurt, hypothermic or disoriented, he might travel in any direction.

John and Melody descended a deep slope into a relatively flat saddle between two rock faces. John was about to suggest a rest break, when his radio crackled. The news was good.

"They found him," he called to Melody, who was poking the snow with her snow poles to be sure the ground ahead was stable.

She turned and came back to where he stood. "Alive?"

"Yes." That one word brought a smile to John's face.

Melody answered with one of her own.

"The chopper is taking the medical team to him now," he went on, the cold and fatigue suddenly not important. "We'll know more when they get there, but the team says the pilot is talking and asking about his boys."

"That's great. Really great." She touched his arm and beamed up at him.

And John, being the idiot he was, gathered her into a bear hug and lifted her high off the ground in jubilant celebration. "We did it, Mel. We found him!"

Melody laughed down at him as happy as he. For once, she didn't resist the closeness as they shared the moment of joyous relief.

John's relief was twofold. First and foremost for the pilot, but also for himself. If the pilot hadn't survived, to John's way of thinking, the responsibility would have rested on the shoulders of his department.

After a minute, Melody's smile faded. She thumped his shoulder. "Put me down."

He didn't want to. She felt good in his arms, for any reason. Slowly, he eased her down, but as she slid against his body, he was reminded once again of their night alone. A yearning rose inside him to be alone with her again.

What was up with that?

When her feet were firmly on the ground, he still didn't release her. Melody stiffened and pushed at his chest. Her jaw clenched. "Back off, North."

Was he some piece of stupid that he couldn't get the message? He let her go.

"Let's head back to base," he said, but he might as well have saved his breath. Melody called to Chili and started off without her teammate. But even with her frosty attitude toward him, John was a happy man. They had a survivor. By the time he and Melody met up with the other rescue teams, the pilot would be on his way to a Boulder hospital and soon reunited with his loved ones.

The reality of how easily the situation could have gone the other way hit him in the heart. Suddenly, he wanted a good, long visit with his mom and dad and a slice of his mother's cherry pie.

He was trudging along at a rapid pace, his mind on the value of family, when a deep cracking noise captured his attention. He frowned, taking a minute to comprehend the sound.

Suddenly, Chili went crazy, spinning and barking in a restless pattern. Melody, fifty yards ahead of him, whirled, her eyes widening. "John? What's wrong?"

He opened his mouth to reply. Too late. Adrenaline slammed into his body with mach force as the ground beneath him disappeared and he tumbled down, down into a black abyss.

CHAPTER TEN

MELODY WATCHED in stunned disbelief as John disappeared before her very eyes. And then she broke into a run, cursing the thick snow that grabbed at her feet, slowing her down.

Blood rushed in her ears, louder than the pounding of her heart. She shouldn't have been so brusque. She should have been nicer to him. He was a good guy. The last good man on the planet.

"Please be okay. Please."

She skidded to a brief halt at the now-opened crevice. Chili crept cautiously to the edge, whining softly. A good twenty feet below she spotted John's red jacket. He lay still, so still. Dear God, what if she lost him? Without another thought, she started down, skidding and sliding and pleading.

"Be alive. Be alive. Please, John, be alive."

Halfway down, she reconsidered the wisdom of her impetuous decision. She should have prepared better before starting the descent.

Too late. She lost her balance on the last ten feet and went down, twisting her ankle. With a cry of pain she landed on top of John's solid body.

His eyes were closed but his chest rose and fell. Thank

God. He was alive, but so very still. Above, in the blinding white, the red dog barked his worry. "Stay, Chili, stay," she called automatically, too concerned with John to deal with the dog. The barking ceased, replaced by a low, constant whine.

Heart slamming against her rib cage, fear a living thing inside her, she ripped off her gloves, cupped John's face in her hands and pleaded, "Wake up. Please wake up."

She couldn't lose him now, not now when she had just begun to believe in the impossible.

He stirred. A murmur, unintelligible, issued from barely moving lips.

Relief coursed through her. He was conscious.

Melody leaned closer, stroking his face, loving the roughness of his unshaven beard against her fingertips. "Are you hurt? Talk to me, John. Tell me what you need."

"A kiss," he whispered, so close to her lips they tingled. "Prince Charming awakens with a kiss from Sleeping Beauty."

Melody jerked upright. "John North! I thought you were dead." She bopped his chest for good measure and then felt horrible for doing so. She was beside herself with worry and he was joking. The man was impossible. Adorably impossible. "I'm sorry. I shouldn't hit you. You may be hurt. Oh, you scared me to death."

John's eyes popped open, the corners crinkling with humor. "I couldn't resist."

"Are you okay, really?" she asked, aware now of what she hadn't notice before—John's body, rock hard and wonderfully powerful beneath hers. She was so terribly tempted to fling herself against him, to kiss him all over and revel in his strength.

As if he'd read her mind, John's arms wrapped around her.

He pulled her close. Her pulse skittered to a halt and then set up a jackhammer rhythm.

"You zipped down that slope as if you cared," he murmured, lips dangerously grazing her ear.

Melody swallowed a lump of nerves and fought for sanity. "Of course I care. I don't want to be stranded with a dead body in the mountains."

His expression serious, he asked, "Is that the only reason?"

A battle raged inside Melody's mind. Somewhere on that slide down the mountain, she'd crossed a border into John North's territory. She'd come over to his side, and every internal sentry she'd set up to protect her hard-won peace was screaming for a halt. Should she tell the truth or guard the fortress?

As always, her fortress won. "I can't imagine what other reason there could be."

And if her voice quivered, she blamed the breathless sound on the tumble.

John's gaze raked her face a long searching minute, as if he didn't believe her. He cupped the side of her face, pushed off her stocking cap that had skewed to one side, letting her hair tumble loose. He swept her hair back with one gloved hand.

"You're not a very good liar," he murmured.

Confused, enticed, comforted, Melody didn't know what to do anymore.

"I don't know what you're talking about—" Before she could finish, he laid his fingers over her lips.

"Hush. For once just shut up and let me look at you."

Melody's heart slammed to a halt inside her chest. This madness had to stop now. They were at the bottom of a cliff, for goodness' sake, and her ankle throbbed painfully. Why would John North or any man, for that matter, want to look at someone like her? The possibilities were terrifying. She pushed his hands aside and sat up. Moving away from his tempting hands, she snatched up her discarded hat.

"We need to get out of here." If her tone was harsh, he was to blame, but oh, how she longed to be back in his arms.

John was quiet for a minute, the beat of silence uncomfortable. She was certain he could hear her heart pounding.

High above, Chili stood on the ridge barking, frantic to discover his master at the bottom of a snowy pit.

John pushed to a stand, brushing the snow from his clothes. "The slope is steep but I think we can manage without calling in reinforcements."

Melody looked upward toward the ridge. A mass of snow had covered the cliff's edge but now that John had fallen through, the way was clear. Steep, but clear. Normally, she'd be up on the narrow ridge in a hurry, but now she wondered if she could make the climb. Her ankle screamed bloody murder.

Using her snow poles for balance, she pulled herself upright. No use worrying North. If she told him, he would do something macho and endearing and chip away another piece of her heart.

Gingerly, she put her foot down, refusing to wince. Pain shot like lightning up her leg. Her whole body stiffened from the stunning assault. She swallowed back a groan.

John whipped around, brown gaze homing in on her face, and then sweeping downward. "What's wrong with your leg?"

So much for keeping her injury to herself. "I twisted my ankle. Nothing serious. Let's go."

He was down on one knee so fast Melody had no time to react. "Let's see."

"No." Leaning heavily on the poles, she pulled her foot back. "Let's go."

The stubborn mule didn't budge. He grabbed her booted foot and held fast. Using his teeth to remove his gloves, he ran his fingers beneath her pant leg and down the back of her calf. None of that hurt. Actually, his hands felt good. But when he rotated her foot ever so gently, she sucked in an inadvertent breath.

"You're injured." His tone was full of reproach, whether for her or himself, she couldn't tell. "You should have told me."

"I'll survive. But we have to get up that slope."

Before Melody could attempt another step, John grabbed his radio and called base, letting them know the situation. When he ordered a chopper, she groaned in humiliation. In fifteen years of working in the mountain wilderness, she had never requested anyone's help.

"I don't need a chopper," she hissed in his ear.

He brushed her away as if she were a housefly. "Executive decision. I'm in command."

"Well, commander, I won't ride in it." She pushed off with the snow poles, started up the incline and with a grunt of pain promptly fell on her behind.

"You will." Hands under her arms John easily stood her upright and held her there. "But we'll have to get ourselves out of this ravine and up on that ridge. Can you manage if I help?"

She hopped on one foot, gingerly touching down with the screaming ankle.

"Of course, I can," she said, not at all confident in her ability to walk, but confident in John North. She didn't want to be, but she was.

"I'll go up first and find a place to secure a rope. Then I'll come back for you. Okay?"

She nodded, feeling stupid and helpless. Over the years, she'd been hurt a few times, but she'd managed on her own. Now, as she watched John North pull himself expertly up the side of a mountain, she had to face the truth. She couldn't do this alone.

By now, her ever faithful dog had gone into a frenzy. Barking like mad, he paced back and forth on the ridge, eager to come down, but obedient to the last command. If she were to die here, Chili would die too, before abandoning her. A sting of unwelcome tears burned her eyes. Could a man ever be that loving?

Before she had time to finish stewing, John descended the slope again, this time with a rope in one hand. Using the rope for balance and leverage, John slid an arm around her waist and helped her walk and hop her way to the top. Once out of the crevice, he swept her into his arms.

"Put me down."

John growled, showing his teeth, and kept trudging through the snow. Fighting took too much effort and her ankle hurt too badly, so Melody gave up the protest, looped her arms around John's neck and laid her head on his shoulder. Just for a moment, she let herself enjoy his protection and care. To a woman who couldn't ever remember being protected, the sensation felt strange, but good. Really, really good.

That's when she decided she must be hypothermic and therefore delirious. She snuggled her cold nose against his warm neck, feeling the powerful punch of his pulse. And just for a moment, while she was delirious and couldn't help herself, Melody wondered what it would be like to be loved by John North. She snuggled closer and pretended she was someone else, someone beautiful and lovable, someone who could love in return.

By the time the chopper arrived, she and John were safely waiting on the ridge and Melody had regained her common sense. Pain and bone-chilling temperatures were a lethal combination. No wonder she'd been delirious.

John paced the waiting room of the Boulder Hospital emergency room. Melody had been furious about the helicopter coming to her rescue and had insisted she did not need a doctor. She'd finally agreed to make the trip to Boulder in John's SUV after the search and rescue teams departed and he'd finished the rounds of questions and reporters. All the while she'd sat in his office unable to escape, so by the time they'd started to Boulder, she'd frozen him with silence.

The woman just didn't understand. He was responsible for her injury and a Ranger never shirked a duty.

And if he'd admit the truth, he saw Melody as far more than a duty. That fact bothered him and he didn't know what to do about it, considering her overall attitude toward him, but there was something about her. At first, he'd been intrigued and had thought her aura of mystery had been the attraction. Then her sensuality, the sexiness against all odds, had started to get to him. And that's where he wanted his feelings to stop. But they didn't.

Admittedly, he wanted to peel back the mysterious layers of Melody Crawford and kiss her until she was out of his system. But something more nagged him like a toothache.

When she'd come tumbling down the side of the cliff as if she cared, all kinds of crazy thoughts had ricocheted around his brain. Her fall had scared him, too. He'd suffered a moment of insanity in which he'd wanted to crush her to him, roll her over in the snow and kiss her until she'd begged for more—or punched him in the nose.

He smiled a little at the thought and crossed the narrow strip of room to peer outside at the postcard-perfect mountains.

When Melody had landed on his chest, teasing her had been too good to resist, and for a minute she'd relaxed in his arms, relieved to find him alive and well. She felt something, too, and it was more than relief. He was sure of it. He had no idea where this thing between them was going, but after today he was determined to find out.

And now, here he was ready to take her back to that empty cabin where not one soul waited to care for her.

The exam room door swooshed open, belching out the scent of antiseptic and the sight of Melody in a wheelchair, her ankle in some type of brace. John's gut twisted. He didn't like seeing her hurt.

A green-clad nurse rolled the chair toward him, smiling. The nurse might look happy, but the patient did not.

"Melody?" he said, going to her. He took her hand and even when she stiffened, he held tight. "What's the verdict?"

"Nothing broken. I'm fine. Take me home."

A typical Melody answer which told him nothing. John resisted an eye roll, looking instead to the smiley nurse for answers.

"Badly torn ligaments," she said, handing him a sheet of instructions. "She needs to stay off that foot for at least three weeks. RICE. Rest, ice, compression and elevation. No weight bearing. Then we'll reevaluate."

John knew the drill. He also knew that Melody would not be an obedient patient. Miss Independence had dogs to train. And she lived alone without anyone to make certain she followed doctor's orders.

Which was exactly why he had come to a conclusion; a conclusion that would undoubtedly set off a major battle. But John North knew how to fight—and win. He had made up his mind and no amount of sputtering or porcupine quills would deter him. Melody needed his help and she was going to get it.

She was about to take on a new cabinmate.

Him.

"You are not staying here."

Melody thought she would faint. And not from the pain of her ankle. John North had some harebrained idea about moving into her cabin while she recuperated from the sprained ankle.

"I owe you," he said, his stubborn jaw clenched tighter than the brace around her foot. "If you hadn't come to my rescue, this wouldn't have happened."

She stared at him as though he'd grown horns and a tail. "I don't want you here."

"Tough."

The moment they'd arrived at her house, he'd deposited her in the fat easy chair in her living room, propped her foot on three pillows stacked on a small table and then made his insane announcement. Now, he stood, fists on hips, expression determined while her body flushed hot and cold and her brain threatened to explode.

"I'll call the police," she warned, knowing she'd do no such thing. John had carried her when she couldn't walk. And she liked him. A lot. That's why he couldn't stay. She couldn't risk it.

She couldn't bear having him underfoot day and night, to see him and talk to him and know she could never, ever have him.

There it was—the truth. She wanted John North for longer than a few days or weeks.

John wasn't deterred by her threat. "I'll have you arrested for stealing my pistol."

She opened her mouth and clapped it shut again, stewing. He knew about the pistol. She should have known he would figure out her subterfuge, but she was surprised he didn't ask what she'd done with the weapon.

"Admit it for once, Melody." His tone gentled. He crouched down beside her chair and took her hand. She wanted to pull away but couldn't. "You can't take care of the animals or even yourself without help. You need me."

God help her. She did need him. Another reason why he couldn't stay. Need begat dependence which begat pain.

"People will talk."

"They already do." He shrugged, a half smile forming crinkles around his mouth. "And you don't care anyway. So get used to me. I'm here and there is not a thing you can do about it."

Melody didn't know how to fight him, and she hated the helpless feeling.

Tears pushed at the back of her eyelids and burned her nose. She didn't cry. She never cried. She hated John North for making her feel things.

No, she didn't. She couldn't hate John. That was the problem.

She squeezed her eyes shut against the emotion and turned her head away.

John didn't move for several minutes. She could feel him watching her. She could hear his steady breathing. Her heart beat in her throat, anxious, but with another, more frightening emotion, too. When she thought her chest would burst, he stood and, with a quiet rustle of denim, moved away.

"I'm going into town to get some things from my house

and to check in at that office again. Do you need anything before I leave?"

She shook her head and refused to look at him. If she ignored him long enough, he would go away.

The door gently snicked shut. An engine revved up. Melody opened her eyes. The room looked empty, bereft even, without him.

"Oh, Ace," she whispered to the German shepherd who had slumped into a sighing heap at her side. "I think we're in big trouble."

CHAPTER ELEVEN

THE FIRST NIGHT ALONE in the cabin with the stubborn as granite John North, Melody laid awake in her tiny bedroom too stressed to sleep. John had collapsed, exhausted, on the living room floor in his sleeping bag and didn't so much as wiggle until the alarm chimed at five in the morning. Chili and Ace, the traitors, had joined him. Until the wee hours of the morning, she'd listened to them breathe and wondered how she would survive the days to come.

When he'd left for the office, Melody pretended to be asleep and then, enticed by the kitchen smells slid out of bed, using crutches to hop into the living room.

The note on the microwave made her laugh. The bold scrawl demanded:

Get off the foot now! Take the pancakes with you. Coffee is ready, too. I'll be back soon. You won't know when to expect me, so don't try to cheat. Stay off the foot! John.

He reappeared at noon with a hamburger and French fries and a book, which he'd tossed on the table next to her chair.

"I have no idea what you like to read. The court clerk next door to my office suggested this."

Melody glanced at the title and suppressed a groan. A romance novel. As if her imagination wasn't already swimming with ideas. When John was gone, she wanted him to come back. When he was there, she wanted him gone.

That night, as she leaned over the bathtub, trying to figure out how to get in and out on one foot, John appeared at the bathroom door. "Got a problem?"

She blushed red-hot. "I thought you were outside."

"Just came in."

"The dogs?" She held to the side of the tub, painfully aware of how small the room had become with John North in it. And how out of place and masculine he looked amidst the green frog and yellow toadstool decor.

"Dogs are okay. I took them for a run."

She pretended a pout. "I'm jealous."

"Don't be. They know I'm not you and are really disappointed. They said so. The border collie told me to take a hike. Alone."

His silliness cheered her. He knew she worried about not being able to maintain the dogs' training regimen. "They love anyone with the feed bucket."

"Not true. Kip didn't even lick me." Kip had the most generous tongue in canine history. John stepped closer, his eyebrows drawing together in a tiny, appealing frown. "Let's get you back to the chair."

She shrank away. "I want to take a bath, but…"

John sized up the situation in two seconds flat. His frown disappeared. "Not a problem. I'll put you into the tub."

Melody shook her head. Was he crazy? "Um, I don't think so."

"Why not?"

"Think about it, North. You're a smart guy. I have to be naked to take a bath."

A slow smile worked its way upward to crinkle the corners of his eyes. He waggled his eyebrows. "I knew that."

A couple of months ago, she would have been scared. Now she fought a ridiculous buzz of energy. "Please go away. I'll figure this out on my own, thank you."

She hopped a couple of times to keep her balance. One of the dogs ambled past the bathroom door and came inside to check things out. He sniffed at John's pant leg.

"I have an idea," John said.

Melody pointed at him. "No."

He grabbed her finger and laughed. "I'll wait outside while you undress and put on your robe. Then I'll lift you into the empty tub and leave again. You can take it from there."

"Oh."

"Good idea, huh?"

"Yes," she conceded.

He stood there.

"Um, are you going to leave or what?"

"Oh, yeah." He started backing out of the narrow room. "I was hoping you'd forget."

"Ha-ha. Go away."

The idea worked brilliantly. After undressing, she donned the robe, tying and retying the cloth belt before calling John's name.

The fact that her bathroom door opened with uncanny speed was not lost on Melody. John had been standing right outside.

With military precision that should have terrified her, he

marched in and swung her over the tub's edge. But the muscles in his arms flexed and bunched in the most inviting manner, she was loath to let go.

Carefully lowering her to a one-footed stand on the green frog appliqués scattered along the bottom of the tub, he ordered, "Grab the wall for balance."

What she really wanted was to grab him for balance.

"Yes, General." She braced a hand against the wall. "I'm good."

He studied her just long enough to make her blush, did an about-face, and marched out. The door snapped shut, unlocked.

Good grief. She was alone in the house with an Army Ranger, naked, one-legged, the door unlocked, and she wasn't on the verge of panic. The old memory tried to push to the forefront, but a new memory gained control. And all during the bath, as water sluiced over her sensitized flesh, she remembered the tender strength of John's hands on her body with only the thin robe and sash between them.

John stretched his long legs inside the Polarfleece sleeping bag as he settled in the darkened living room for another night on Melody's floor. He didn't mind. He'd slept in far worse circumstances.

Canine toenails tapped on the wood flooring. From the careful steps, he recognized Ace who slumped down beside him with an *oomph* and a sigh. John poked one hand outside the bag to rest on the warm German shepherd. Somewhere along the line the dog had bonded to him, and though Melody was clearly Ace's master and best friend, John had grown fond of the animal.

He'd grown fond of the animal's owner, as well. That first

night when he'd carried her from the bathtub, she'd smelled like heaven and looked adorably sexy in her Pooh Bear pajamas. Warm and soft from the heat of the bath, her face and neck had flushed the color of summer roses. She'd looked incredibly young and his chest had swelled with an overpowering need to take care of her.

He figured the emotion was a good sign. He was, after all, responsible for what happened to her.

Somehow though, when he held Melody in his arms, he had trouble thinking of her as a duty.

The truth was he liked being here with her. For all her sputtering, she could be sweet and funny and warm. She was smart, too, giving him ideas for improving the department that he would not have considered otherwise. She took his mind off the department troubles, too. After the plane crash, someone had leaked a couple of negative stories to the press. He suspected the culprit but had no evidence.

Time spent with Melody each evening both cheered and challenged him. He had feelings for her. Deeper feelings than he ever thought possible. Now he was determined to discover what mysteries lay beneath the fascinating surface of Melody Crawford. All she needed was a little encouragement from the right source. And he intended to be that source.

By midweek, Melody was on the verge of combustion. John North had invaded her space and she was growing dependant upon him, both physically and emotionally. Every day he did something that endeared him more. She'd never expected to long for a man's company the way she did for John's. What was she going to do when he left for good?

Balancing on crutches, she hobbled to the cheval mirror to

comb her hair. As always, it flopped in shaggy disarray around her face. Hopeless. She would never be the kind of woman a man found attractive. Even if she wanted to be.

The picture on the dresser smiled at her. A happy military family. Mom and Dad and Jacob and Melody. She missed her family. She missed Jacob's ornery teasing, his imitations of Jim Carrey. And Mom had been the one who'd taught her to quilt. She'd patiently tolerated her little girl's crooked, oversize stitches.

Then there was Dad. She'd loved him so much. He'd been her hero. She turned her face away and refused to look at the tall, dark soldier. Daddies were supposed to take care of their families. He should have protected them.

The bullets had killed everyone but her. She still didn't understand why she'd survived the brain surgery, the coma and months of rehabilitation while the others had died at the scene.

She resisted the urge to touch the scar. Instead, she swung her crutches toward the kitchen to put on a pot of stew. Her ankle throbbed and started to swell again. John would scold.

Her mood lifted at the thought of big, tough John wagging his finger in her face and scolding like a second grade teacher. She smiled a little.

Hours later, John arrived bearing a laptop and a load of paperwork. Sure enough he scolded.

"You've been up too much." He stood at the end of her chair, hands on hips, staring down at her propped foot. It was puffy and bruised.

Melody glanced up from her latest romance novel. She was starting to like these things. "Nag."

"Hardhead," he said, but the retort lacked energy. He looked beat.

Melody was glad she'd prepared dinner.

"You work too hard," she said, and then blushed. She sounded like a fretting wife.

Waving off the suggestion he went to the table and flipped open the laptop. "Reports, grants, job descriptions, emergency plans, talks to civic groups and schools. The paperwork never ends."

"You can't be sleeping well on my floor. Really, John. I'm okay. Why don't you go home?"

He poked a key on the computer and didn't look up. "I'm needed here. You're my responsibility."

Is that what she was? "I don't want to be."

With a terrible certainty, Melody knew she wanted to be something but not a responsibility.

"Tough."

She gave up the argument. "Any news on the plane crash victims?"

The computer played a tune. John tilted the screen away. "Doing fine. The newspapers are all over it. Apparently, the dad is running for some state office."

"I'm glad they're okay. How are things otherwise?"

"The same old stuff. Clausen's still making waves. He thinks I'm not handling the job."

"That's ridiculous. You're the best thing to happen to this area in years. Without your leadership the pilot and his sons would be dead."

"Why thank you, Melody. I think that was a compliment."

She blushed, but her face glowed with a sincerity that touched John. He didn't tell her the rest. That someone had started a rumor about the two of them, claiming John was shirking his duty because of her. He wasn't. He worked darned hard to keep up with everything, including his responsibility to the woman beside him.

Screw Tad Clausen and his dirty, jealous mind. Squinting at the laptop, he squeezed his temples between thumb and forefinger.

"Headache?" Melody asked quietly. At some point, she'd gotten up from her chair and come to stand beside him. He'd make her sit down in a minute but right now, her nearness cheered him.

"Starting." He rotated his shoulders. "Tension."

Melody hobbled to the bathroom, returning with two pain relievers. "These will help."

The sweet gesture squeezed him right in the center of his chest. It occurred to him then that at some point Melody had gone from wanting to tear his head off to this. A wall had come down. She was letting him see the real person behind the porcupine quills.

And he liked her even more.

If he hadn't already been through the love wringer once before and come out smashed and broken... Well, he had. So that was that.

"You need to get off your foot," he said, more to stop his own thinking than anything. She ignored him.

Instead, Melody waited for him to down the pills, then maneuvered around behind the chair and did something completely out of character. She began massaging his shoulders, tentatively at first, and then when he didn't protest, more vigorously.

She leaned in, her body braced against his. The scent of her, clean as soap but way more appealing, battled with the warmth of tomatoey beef stew bubbling on the stove.

The combination of scent and touch and relief was sensory overload. He thought he'd die from pleasure.

His head lolled. "That feels amazing."

She kneaded the knot twisted inside his trapezoid muscles. "You're tight as a fiddle string."

Oh, yeah. He was tight in any number of places, the band around his heart being the worst.

"Try this one." John pushed a green-and-blue jigsaw puzzle piece toward Melody's side of the coffee table.

She still couldn't believe she'd massaged his shoulders, but he'd looked so miserable she'd thought nothing of the simple, comforting action. Then, as she'd stroked his muscles, listened to his sighs and touched the place at the back of his neck where his dark hair grew in a fascinating swirl, her mind had gone crazy again. She'd wanted an excuse to be in his arms. Which really was insane. He'd told her she was nothing but a responsibility. And that's the way she wanted things to be. They were nothing to each other. Nothing.

Then why was he still here? And why did she love the sound of his voice? Why did she notice the way he stirred his coffee and the way his chambray shirts stretched across his shoulders?

She frowned, trying to concentrate on the puzzle. "There are too many greens and blues."

"What did you expect from a five-thousand-piece picture of a Hawaiian rain forest?"

"Too true." She took the piece and turned it several different directions before laying it aside again. "Won't fit, but thanks anyway."

John had taken up residence on the small couch next to her

chair. She felt him there, too close, even when he wasn't helping with the puzzle. He was supposed to be doing paperwork, but a few minutes ago, he'd shut the laptop.

"How's your headache?" she asked.

He rotated his shoulders. "Better, thanks to you. Tension's a killer."

An understatement if ever she heard one. The tension between them was killing her.

"Did you finish your work?"

"The stack never ends. I still need to enter all the data you and I collected. Maybe tomorrow night."

"Couldn't I do that for you?"

He shrugged her off. "I'll get to it eventually."

"Oh, well, if you'd rather."

"Do you want to?"

With a sigh, she plunked down her puzzle piece and admitted, "I need to be working."

"You need to heal up."

"You're not hearing me. I *need* to work. I need the money." There, she'd admitted it. "Ace's surgery cost more than I could afford. And since we aren't able to work in the field, I thought maybe—" She shrugged, letting the thought die, embarrassed to have him know her financial woes.

Before she realized what he was up to, John smoothed her hair away from her face. "You're on paid leave."

She tensed, afraid he'd see the scar and ask questions. "How can I be? I didn't work for the department long enough to accumulate leave."

"Injured on the job." A nerve over his cheekbone twitched. What was he not saying?

"I'd feel a lot better about this if you'd let me help with the paperwork. I like to stay busy, John. Sitting around here with my leg in the air is driving me crazy." *And so are you.*

"Well, in that case, be my guest. I'm sick of the computer."

"You'll have to show me how." Her breath caught at the idea of huddling close to the computer with John.

"Sure. It's easy. I'll show you and then you can enter the data anytime you're bored."

"Which is pretty much every second except when I'm re-habbing Ace's knees."

Ace, who was stretched in front of the coffee table, raised his head in question.

"He seems to be coming along pretty well." John reached around her to snap a puzzle piece into place. While her thoughts had been on him, he'd been studying the puzzle. *Annoying man.*

The newly formed section looked a lot like a tree limb.

"He's doing better than I am." She wiggled her foot for emphasis.

"I find that shade of navy blue rather fetching," John said, reaching to tweak her big toe. "Did anyone ever mention you have pretty feet?"

She curled her toes inward to hide them, wishing she owned some nail polish. "Don't be silly."

"I'm serious. Pretty feet, great legs, gorgeous face."

The compliment floored her. John thought she was pretty?

Even an hour later, John couldn't get past Melody's reaction to a simple compliment.

He was in the dog kennel, giving each of the animals a little TLC. Darkness had fallen like a rock and the night air was still and bracing. He latched the pen and started toward the house, his hands shoved deep in his pockets.

His little dog trainer had no idea how exotically lovely she was.

His. He'd thought of her as his. Considering last night's conversation, he'd better rethink. The independent lady would hate him if she discovered he was the one paying her salary. She'd be insulted and angry and send him packing. But he refused to stop. She needed the money. He needed her help.

And Melody needed to understand how special she was.

He made a detour to his truck and another to the storage building. Then he went inside for Melody.

"Bundle up," he said, tossing the blue-and-orange ski suit into her lap. "We're going outside."

If he'd known her face would light up this way, he'd have taken her outside every night.

While she struggled into warm outerwear, he roamed in and out of the house, setting things up to ensure her comfort.

When he swept her into his arms for the journey outside, she asked, "What are we doing?"

"A surprise."

"What kind of surprise?"

He snapped off the light, kicked the back door closed and carried her out into the pitch-black darkness. "Trust me. You'll like it."

"Mmm. Mysterious." For once, Melody didn't argue or insist he put her down. When he lowered her to the waterproof blanket he'd placed on the ground, John was reluctant to let her go.

Melody loved the outdoors as much as he and the complete darkness of a mountain night didn't bother her at all. In fact, she relished it.

"Snuggle up." Keeping things light, John covered them both with a fluffy thermal blanket. "And look up."

Melody lay back and stared up at the inky, star-spangled sky. "This is beautiful."

"Just wait. It gets better." He grinned to himself, glad his job required a close monitoring of weather and atmosphere.

The night air was clear and cold and as crisp as a potato chip. He puffed a ring of smoke vapor and pointed, "There's the Big Dipper."

"And Orion's Belt." Her arm came up to rest alongside his. Instinctively, he scooted closer, leaning his head next to hers so that they were both gazing in the same direction. He wanted to absorb every nuance of her reaction when the meteor shower began. He hoped she loved it as much as he thought she would.

She didn't disappoint him. With the first streak of light across the sky, she gasped. "John, look. A shooting star."

His lips curved in a smile.

"Oh. Another one." She grabbed his deltoid and squeezed, gaze never leaving the sky. "John, look at that. Oh, my goodness. Another one. It's a meteor shower."

The grin inside his chest spread, warmer than a June day. Melody was like a kid in a toy store, all agog over nature's wonder. He turned his head, more interested in watching her than in watching the heavenly light display. Her face went through a gamut of emotions—excitement, wonder, delight.

Emotion squeezed the breath from him as he studied the curve of her cheekbone, watched her exotic eyes widen, listened to her sweet cries of pleasure.

Melody suddenly raised up on her elbow. Without warning, she kissed his cheek.

"Thank you," she murmured, breath warm against his skin. "This was the best night of my life."

The simple admission crumbled him.

A woman like Melody was a rare gift. Give her diamonds in the sky and she was happy.

Unable to resist, he pulled her into his arms, throbbing with the desire to shower her with far more than falling stars. But she was fragile, sometimes afraid, and her fear both angered and destroyed him. What had happened to this special lady? Who had crushed her tender spirit and left her afraid and alone?

He wanted to heal her hurt and erase her fear. He wanted to kiss her and hold her and love her. And he couldn't understand why he didn't go ahead and do it.

The realization struck like an asteroid. He was afraid to kiss her again, because if he did, he might discover he was helplessly in love with Melody Crawford.

CHAPTER TWELVE

"Melody."

Melody rested her head on John's chest. His words skimmed the top of her hair with breathy warmth.

Hoping for a few more falling stars, they remained beneath the cozy blanket staring up at the Milky Way. Relaxed and mellowed by the pleasure of the event, Melody was deeply moved that John had somehow known how much a night beneath the falling stars would mean to her.

"Umm-hmm?" she said, lazily.

A beat of time passed, and then, "Who broke your heart?"

Melody's blood chilled. "What?"

One of John's strong fingers played in her hair, twirling aimlessly, a calm counterpoint to the intense question. "Who made you afraid? What happened to drive you up here all by yourself?"

Tightness constricted her breathing. In the years since she'd left Denver behind and moved to Granny's cabin, she'd never told anyone.

"I don't know what you mean."

His chest rose and fell in a sad, gusty sigh. "Can't you just this once trust me with the truth?"

"I don't know." The words were a worried whisper.

"You can trust me with anything, sweetheart. I'm not going to hurt you. I'd never hurt you."

For some fathomless reason, Melody believed him.

As hard as she'd fought against the feelings, she was in love with John North. He had been good to her even when she'd behaved like a witch to drive him away. He'd stroked her battered ego, nurtured her wounded soul, teased and touched and talked until she'd fallen in love with him.

Did she dare let down her wall of defense and trust him with the worst?

"Why?" she asked, stalling.

He stirred slightly and she felt his confusion. "Why what? I don't understand."

"Why should I trust you?"

"Because I—" Again, that hesitancy. Another sigh. And then, "Because I'm a man of my word. I take responsibility very seriously."

Her hope faltered. She was in love with him, and he considered her a responsibility. So be it. Responsibility was actually better than love. Love hurt too much.

"I know you do."

"Then tell me what's wrong. I want to help."

"No one can help, John. What's done is done. All the compassionate thoughts in the world can't bring back my family." She sat up, pulling away from his warmth to hug her knees.

"I thought this might have something to do with your family." When she didn't respond, he sat up, too, moving close to her side. He bumped her shoulder with his. "You never talk about them. What happened?"

Anxiety rattled inside her like rocks in a tin can. "Maybe we shouldn't have this conversation."

She started to get up. John stopped her with a hand on her arm. "Don't run from me, Melody."

Run. Retreat. Escape. She'd been running for years and she was soul weary.

A pair of coyotes yipped somewhere nearby. The dogs in the kennel stirred, restless at the sound, and one of them *woofed* once in warning.

Melody relaxed again. Why not tell him? What possible harm could come of it?

"My family is dead," she said simply. "All of them at once."

"An accident?"

She made an angry huffing sound.

"Murder is never an accident." The harsh word shimmied on the air, almost visible in its stark ugliness. "I was supposed to die with them. I did die, in a way. Nothing was ever the same again after that night."

John stirred, agonized by the haunted quality in her voice, but he knew when to keep his mouth shut and listen. Anything he said now could stop the flow of words.

"We were all asleep when the murderer came in," she said softly, speaking into the shielding darkness, her profile a pale specter in the starlight. "A popping noise woke me up. I was scared but I didn't know why. Instinct, I guess. I knew something bad was happening. I heard another pop. And then footsteps. My bedroom door opened. And he came in. I could barely see him in the dark. He was a shadow, a nightmare. I was so scared I slid down in the bed, hoping he'd go away. I knew something was terribly, terribly wrong."

Melody shuddered and put her forehead on her upraised knees. Her breath came hard and fast as though she'd run up a mountain.

John couldn't stand it. He touched her hair. "Mel…"

"A gun feels so cold and hard against your temple." Her voice went somewhere far away as if he didn't exist and she was talking to herself. "I never heard the explosion. But I saw it somehow behind my eyelids. A blast of radiating light and then darkness. After that I didn't know anything for a very long time. He killed us all. Mama, Jacob, me and himself."

John squeezed his eyes shut against her raw and naked pain. "Who, baby? Who did this to your family?"

"A soldier. A brave, brave hero. A good man who lost his mind. Everyone said so."

No wonder she'd reacted so strongly to his military background.

"Did you know him?"

He heard her gulp back a sob and ached to take her in his arms. But right now, she held herself rigid and alone and he feared she'd break like fragile crystal if he touched her. He almost wished he hadn't asked. When she finally answered, he understood her sense of betrayal.

"Oh, yes, I knew him. He was my father." A powerful shudder convulsed her slim shoulders. "My own daddy. He killed us all. Even himself. They called it post-traumatic stress. Said he didn't know what he was doing. But we were all dead just the same."

And then she broke. Like an injured child, she began to weep.

The horror of what she'd been through overwhelmed him. He'd been in battle, he'd seen horrors, but not like this. Not this kind of betrayal by someone who was supposed to love him. Now he understood the wall of protection she had erected around herself.

"Let me hold you, Melody. Please. I need to hold you."

Those must have been the words she needed to hear. She turned and let him draw her into the warm, tender circle of his protection.

She cried for a very long time, until John thought his heart would rip right out of his chest. He knew about PTSD and the troubling, sometimes tragic results. All the knowledge in the world didn't make Melody's sorrow any less painful to witness.

"Shh. Sweetheart. Shh. Don't cry. You're killing me. I can't stand to hear you cry." He rocked her back and forth, soothing, murmuring, making promises to take care of her. "No one will ever hurt you again. Not as long as I have breath."

The temperature had fallen and she was shivering, both from cold and emotion. He slowly laid her back against the blanket, tucking it beneath her chin. He kissed her forehead as he would a child. She lifted her arms and reached for him. He didn't resist. He slid with her beneath the cover and stretched above her, kissing her tears away.

He'd meant only to comfort but after a long time when her tears had ceased, he continued to kiss her eyelids, her cheeks, her forehead. His body quivered to erase all her heartache and give her only good memories.

He moved to kiss her chin. She turned her head ever so slightly. "Kiss me, John. For real."

His heart slam-dunked against his rib cage.

"Whatever the lady wants," he whispered as their lips met.

The kiss began with the tender throb of emotion. He didn't want to scare her or hurt her. But when her lips parted to take him in, John deepened the kiss, letting her know how much she affected him and how much he wanted her. Fireworks went off behind his eyelids. The fever in his blood grew more insistent.

"Let's go in the house," he murmured.

She shook her head, tugging his face back down for another mind-numbing kiss. "No. Please."

If they didn't go in now, they might be out here all night, because he was fast losing his usual rigid self-control.

"You're cold."

When she didn't deny it, he rose, lifting her with him and carried her into the bedroom.

The side of the bed dipped with John North's weight as he placed her on the bed and followed her down.

Melody gulped back the wave of anxiety. She wanted this. She wanted John North. But she wanted far more than a one-night stand brought about through sympathy.

This could go no further. She had to stop.

John kissed her again, and she almost changed her mind. John North's mouth on hers was like the man himself—manly and hard, but tender and in control.

He'd promised to keep her safe. He would never hurt her. She was so tired of feeling afraid.

But right now, her emotions were everywhere, scattered and overwrought. A decision to be with John had greater ramifications than she was able to deal with tonight. She couldn't let this happen, no matter how much she loved this fine man.

"John," she murmured, a hand to his lips so he couldn't kiss her again.

He pushed her hand aside and kissed her anyway.

"John, stop."

From his instant reaction, she'd said the magic word. He froze, suspended above her, brown eyes melting her with their intensity. "I want to make love to you."

Her pulse bumped. "I know. But I can't. Not now. Not like

this. I'm too scattered, too drained." She touched his tense jaw. "I'm sorry. Please don't be angry."

She wanted the first time with John to be beautiful and special, not an exhausted, confused coupling. And certainly not on the night she'd discussed the murders. Murder and love, as she well knew, did not go together.

John groaned and pressed his forehead against hers. "I'm not angry, sweetheart. Frustrated maybe. Not angry."

Her sigh was filled with relief and more than a little regret as John rolled to the edge of the bed and sat up. She placed a hand on his muscled back.

"I'm sorry," she said. "Thank you for not pushing me."

"I told you." He rubbed his face hard with both hands. "You can trust me. I'd die before I'd hurt you."

And though caution born of trauma warned her to be careful, she believed him.

After a quiet moment, her beloved stood and went to the door. She ached to call him back for a good-night kiss, but anything more would be unfair to him.

"John."

He turned, a tall shadow in the doorway. But this shadow emanated compassion and kindness, not murder. And she was not afraid.

"Thank you for tonight. For everything."

He smiled, gave her a slow salute and closed the door.

And she loved him even more for understanding.

Long after the house quieted, Melody remained awake, staring up at the play of faint moonlight on her ceiling. Over and over, the video in her head replayed the evening with John North. He had given her the magical star-gazing as a gift she would always cherish. With that one simple gesture, he'd made her happy. He'd even fed her marshmallows and hot chocolate when the night had grown long and cold.

When he'd listened with compassion to her story, the revelation had somehow taken the edge off her shame and sorrow. Enough that she'd begun to believe in the impossible. In this one magical evening, her dead heart had come to life. Perhaps she should have made love with him. He'd given her so much tonight and she'd given nothing in return.

She glanced at the illuminated clock at her bedside. Morning would arrive soon. John would get very little sleep again tonight.

She heard him stir. Was he still awake?

Pushing back the thick comforter, she painstakingly limped into the living room. John had pulled the fat, easy chair close to the furnace and propped his feet on the ottoman.

In sleep, the lines around his mouth relaxed, but she saw his fatigue. He worked so hard and now she'd kept him up half the night again.

He'd sacrificed a great deal to stay here with her. Why had he done that? Did his feelings for her extend beyond responsibility?

The memory of his rough voice saying, "I want to make love to you," shimmied over her skin like warmed velvet. Love. Was the word only a euphemism for sex? Or something more?

She stood beside the chair, staring down into his face. She hadn't believed it was possible for her to love anyone again. And yet, here she stood, loving John North and wishing for him to love her in return. His eyelids fluttered and she thought he might wake. Instead he moaned, caught in a dream. She watched his rugged features contort and wondered what he dreamed. His head tossed to one side.

"No," he mumbled. "Get back. Get back."

He thrashed. His fists tightened at his sides as the dream deepened, taking him to some terrible place. He'd been in combat. He must have seen far more frightening things than she had. And she'd seen her share of blood and death.

He called out again and Melody's chest pinched with sadness. She didn't want him to suffer. Not ever. Not even in sleep.

"John." She touched his shoulders.

His eyes flew open, wild and unseeing. Reflexively, Melody shrank back.

"John," she said. "Wake up."

In the next instant her body slammed against the wall, John's powerful forearm shoved high and tight into her windpipe.

She stared down in shock. And then in terror.

The fearsome warrior towered above her like a madman, ready to kill.

Melody screamed…and shattered into a thousand pieces.

John was yanked out of one nightmare and catapulted into another. He'd been fighting a soldier to keep him from hurting Melody. Melody was screaming. He had to save her.

He came wide-awake.

Oh, no.

"Melody." He jerked his arm away from her soft throat, slapping the light switch at the same time.

Melody crumpled like burning paper. He caught her before she hit the floor.

What had he done?

"Melody, sweetheart." He fell to his knees with her in his arms.

She fought him. "Get away from me."

What could he do? He released her. She scrambled to the other side of the room and stood glaring at him, chest heaving.

How did he make up for this? "I'm sorry. I never meant to hurt you."

"You promised. You promised," she sobbed.

He had. "I was dreaming. I didn't know. I was dreaming about you—"

She didn't let him finish. She chopped the air with one arm.

"No. Get away from me." Shaking convulsively, she wound both arms protectively around her body. "Leave me alone."

Hands outstretched, he took two steps toward her. "Not until you listen to me."

"I want you gone. Out of my house." She jabbed a trembling finger toward the door. "Now."

John dropped back, stung by her vehemence.

"I won't leave you like this." He went to the sink and ran a glass of water. "Sit down. Calm down."

She only stood there, glaring as though he was her family's murderer.

John tossed back the glass of water, washing down some of his bitter regret, then ran another glass, placing it on the table. "Sit."

Though he was dying to comfort her, he pulled out a chair and sat down to wait. He would go, but not until he knew she would be all right.

After a long painful silence while both dogs moved around the room in curious unrest, Melody's stance changed. Her shoulders relaxed and she uncrossed her arms.

"Please talk to me," he said, his heart breaking.

"This is never going to work." Very slowly, she crossed the room and pulled out a chair. John considered this progress.

"I didn't mean to scare you. Do you believe that?"

She thought about it for too long. When she nodded, he knew she was lying. What was the use? She would never trust him enough. No matter how hard he tried or how much he cared.

"You're right. I should go."

Uncertainty skittered over her face. For a moment, he hoped. And then she nodded.

Chest burning with the fire of regret, John wanted to say so many things, but Melody didn't want to hear them.

Leaving her sitting at the table in self-imposed exile, he went to gather his belongings. He had his sleeping bag rolled and tied when his cell phone broke the painful silence.

Standing rigid and empty, he flipped the device open and barked into the mouthpiece.

His gut tightened another notch.

As if his night couldn't get any worse, they had a call out. Sometime in the night, a child had wondered away from an RV camp and disappeared.

CHAPTER THIRTEEN

HE'D TOLD HER NOT TO COME.

John looked up from the circle of rescue teams he was briefing as Melody limped into the fire station, face pale, grim and determined—no crutches in sight.

Stubborn woman didn't listen. He had to admire her grit and her compassion, though. Her ankle was not completely healed, and yet, even after the ugly scene between the two of them, she was here for the lost child.

His heart lurched, but he tamped back the rush of emotion. She'd tossed him out and he was done. Finished. He'd finally learned his lesson this time. He was darn tired of trying to prove himself to her and the governor and this town.

He scraped a hand over his whisker-roughened face. Truth was, he was just plain tired, but he had a mission and a mission came first. Before his emotions. Before his fatigue.

The briefing completed, John hooked a pen onto his pocket and stormed across the room to Melody. The sooner she was gone, the better. He didn't have time to focus on personal issues today and if she was around, he'd be thinking about her. "You can't search on that ankle."

Her chin hitched. "I'm fine."

"Right." He leaned into her face. "Didn't I have to carry you to bed last night?"

She jerked back, insulted. He was angry and feeling mean. He shouldn't have said that.

"I'm going to search," she snapped, eyes narrowed. "Deal with it."

Several groups of vehicle and foot searchers were preparing to leave. A full unit of dog handlers would arrive within the hour, but Melody and Chili were here now. Even solo, they were the best he'd ever seen. He didn't want her out there on that ankle but if he refused to assign her a sector, she'd go on her own. Then he'd have no idea where she was and her safety would be compromised. She may have broken his heart, but he would die before he'd let anything bad happen to her. He'd promised that much, and even if she didn't believe his promises, he'd keep them anyway.

"Clausen is coordinating assignments." He jabbed a thumb over his shoulder toward the deputy sheriff who held court at a table near the coffeemaker. To John's way of thinking, letting Clausen play team leader would keep him happy and useful, so he'd delegated the task of coordinating teams and assigning sectors to the deputy.

Melody gave him a look of mild reproach but said nothing. John knew she disliked Tad Clausen. But she disliked him, too. If she was going to volunteer, she'd have to deal with both of them.

With a gentle command to the dog, she walked away.

John stood for ten seconds watching her, scowling at the limp she tried to hide. His gut twisted in a knot.

What had happened between them last night? From start

to finish, the evening had been both beautiful and terrible, and he'd had no time to process any of it.

A call came in from the campground where the child was last seen. John shook off thoughts of Melody and hurried to the telephone. He had to get his mind clear and concentrate on the search.

As he finished the phone conversation, someone called his name. Before responding, he shot a brief glance toward the assignment table and saw Tad talking to Melody. Her face was like a stone. He shouldn't have sent her over there with that jerk after what happened last time.

He started in their direction.

"Mr. North." The dispatcher's voice stopped him. "The highway patrol is on the telephone. They want to discuss the chopper situation."

John did an about-face to take the outstretched telephone. Several people from the campground where the child had gone missing had arrived and needed to be interviewed. As operational chief, every single piece of information was filtered through him. By the time he'd fielded another dozen questions and two more calls, he spotted Melody and her dog heading for the exit.

"Excuse me," he said to one of the interviewees. "I'll be right back."

He caught up to Melody and grabbed hold of her arm.

"Melody, I—" he started and then let the thought drop when she shifted around to stare at him with those haunting, betrayed eyes.

She carefully disengaged her arm and stepped back. "I'm on my radio. Unit one."

A thousand thoughts raced through his head. He loved her.

He needed her in his life. She could trust him. But no matter his personal feelings, the mission came first.

"Be careful," he finally said.

For a nanosecond, Melody's stiff attitude crumpled. Some emotion flickered and died on her lovely face. He could swear she wanted to mend the rift between them as badly as he.

But as quickly as the expression came, it disappeared, so that he almost wondered if he had been a victim of his own wishful thinking.

She murmured to the dog and pushed through the glass double doors and out into the gray blustery day.

John stood for several more seconds until she disappeared from sight. He had a bad feeling about this. A real bad feeling. And there was not a thing he could do about it.

Two hours into the search, Melody's ankle shot pain all the way up to her eyeballs. The headache she'd had since she and John argued had become a drumbeat of self-recriminations. She rubbed at her temples.

Had she overreacted to his nightmare?

She didn't know. The harsh reality that John had actually attacked her played over and over inside her head. He'd thrown her against a wall. She could still imagine the press of his powerful arm against her windpipe.

She shivered at the memory. All the fear of the past had culminated in those few moments. She'd behaved like a maniac, practically accusing him of trying to murder her. John probably thought she was insane.

Maybe she was.

Even if she could get past the fear, John was gone from her life for good. No man would tolerate her irrational behavior for long. Making the break was a good thing. Really. It was. She didn't need John North or anyone else. She'd been fine for years. Fine.

Then why did she hurt so much inside that she wanted to lie down in a snowbank and never get up again?

With the grit that had kept her going when her family died, Melody shook off the melancholy. A child was lost. A precious, innocent child.

As she lumbered through the snowy woods and traversed a slick, rocky incline packed hard with ice and snow, she forced her mind to the search. Chili trotted back, eyes bright and interested, but a little worried. He was starting to stress from lack of progress.

Melody opened the plastic bag from her backpack and withdrew a small pink sock with a kitten embroidered on the cuff. The sight twisted and turned inside her. Kylie, the little lost girl, had worn the sock yesterday.

Holding the garment to Chili's incredible nose, she said, "Find Kylie, boy. Find Kylie."

Chili charged off again, but his energy was beginning to flag. From his behavior, Melody was almost sure the child had not come this way, but she was assigned this sector and until it was cleared or the search was called off, she'd stay the course.

Her radio crackled, causing a jump start to her pulse. For a second, she hoped the caller was John. Foolish, she knew. She and John were over. Over before they'd started.

But last night had been magical—for a while. Up until that terrifying moment against the wall Melody had almost believed in the impossible. For a few wonderful hours, she'd dreamed of love and marriage and babies with John North.

Foolish, foolish woman.

The radio crackled again.

Annoyed to have her thoughts constantly distracted with the memories, Melody pushed Talk. "Unit one."

"Melody. Deputy Clausen here. Where are you?"

A curl of distaste made her answer short, but she told him. "Any progress?"

"Nothing. I don't think the child came this way."

"Agreed. Let's move you to another location."

Melody frowned at the black handheld before pressing her mouth close to the speaker. "Leave this sector incomplete?"

Pulling off an unsearched sector wasn't the normal mode of operations but perhaps Tad trusted her dog's judgment. He rattled off a new set of directions, off the grid, farther up the mountain that could be reached only by foot or helicopter.

The climb and rugged terrain would tax her ankle, but she agreed to take on the task. She wanted to find that child.

Calling Chili back to her side, she leashed him, offered a treat and a few minutes rest. Then they started the long climb.

More than halfway up, she slipped, turning her weak ankle. The pain stole her breath. With a cry, she sat down, panting. Snow had begun to fall, not unusual, but distracting and dangerous. A new snow would hamper rescue efforts and make the journey back to base increasingly difficult.

Chili, who had ventured much farther, must have heard Melody's pained cry because he returned again, tail wagging as if to say, "What's up, Mama?"

Struggling to her feet, Melody rubbed the dog's ears to reassure him while she considered what to do. She didn't have to remove her boot to know she'd reinjured the ankle. Already, the boot tightened painfully from renewed swelling, and the throb was enough to bring tears.

Though hating to admit defeat, she had no other choice. She was useless now and to go farther would be treacherous and foolhardy. Calling in, she reported to Tad Clausen and started back to base.

Her backpack seemed to gain weight with every step. She leaned on her probing stick and trudged on. The snow increased. Melody hoped someone would find the little girl soon.

John wouldn't give up. She was sure of that.

Thoughts of John intervened again, filling her aching head with all the might-have-beens and what-ifs. What if they'd made love? What if he hadn't had the nightmare?

From somewhere behind her came a rumbling sound. Adrenaline ratcheted through her body like lightning. She knew that sound. Avalanche.

Ankle screaming in protest, she began to run.

And then her world went from blinding white to cold and black.

John paced the fire station like a caged cougar, stopping to glare at a large, circular clock on the wall. Little Kylie had been found by a hiker some time ago. All the search units had reported in. Most were back at the station by now and some had even gone home. All but one. Melody.

Where the heck was she?

He tried her radio for the third time. No answer.

He knew she was ticked off at him, but no reasonable, ethical search and rescue volunteer would refuse to answer her radio calls because of personal conflict. Would she?

Of course not. Tad hadn't heard from her, either. And he was in command of the ground crews.

John took a ham sandwich from a white pasteboard box

and chomped down, thinking. Until all team members were accounted for, he couldn't rest. And when that team member was Melody—she had to be found.

He tried the radio once again and when Melody still did not answer, went to consult with Clausen. True to form, the deputy was leaning on the back of a pickup truck talking to a reporter. The man loved reporters.

"Deputy Clausen," John said. "Could I have a minute?"

The deputy flashed an easy, dismissing smile at the reporter. "You'll have to excuse me. Official business."

John didn't have the patience to wait for the reporter to leave. He said to Tad, "Have you heard from Melody?"

"Melody?" Tad pretended not to understand. He removed his aviator sunglasses, held them up to the light to examine a smudge.

"All the teams have reported in except her."

Clausen puffed a breath on the lens and rubbed the glasses against his uniform. "Oh, you mean the spooky dog woman."

"Have you heard from her?"

"Well, now, let's see." He slid the glasses in place and turned a "possum-eating" grin to John. "I'd have to check the log to be sure."

The deputy was trying his best to get to him, and if he wasn't careful, Tad would succeed. Already tense, John managed to keep his temper as he ground out, "Then check it. *Now.*"

One golden eyebrow jacked in amusement. "Getting antsy about your little…playmate?"

John's patience meter had just about run out of quarters. "Now is not the time, Clausen. She's been out too long on that bad ankle. Get me the call log."

Deputy Clausen took his sweet time sauntering into the fire

station to the table where radio communications transpired. Before he could flip through the list of calls, John yanked the tablet from his hand.

"There's only one call here from Melody."

"She's not that communicative."

True enough. And she disliked Clausen.

"Where was she when she called in?"

"Leaving her sector."

"Was she headed back to base? Did she know the child was found?"

When Clausen didn't reply, a bad feeling crept up John's spine. "Look, Deputy, we have a responsibility to all our volunteers, whether you like them or not."

"*We* have a responsibility? Excuse me, *Director* North, but you're the man in charge. Any problems that arise are on you, buddy. Not me."

The fact that Tad was gloating about problems arising tuned John's antenna. Something was wrong here. And Clausen knew more than he was saying. "Where is she?"

"You find her. You're the big, tough Army Ranger with all the smarts."

Tamping back the need to smash Tad's pretty nose, John stalked to the assignment map, frantically searching for Melody's assigned sector. He jabbed an index finger at a spot. "She's here, right?"

"Maybe. Maybe not." Tad shrugged, enjoying his power play.

John had about reached his toleration limit. He glared down into the shorter man's face. "Spit it out, Deputy. If you know something say so. And do it quick. I'm tired. And you're already on my last nerve."

"Tired?" Tad smirked. "As in up all night with the lady?"

John pressed closer, pent-up anger and stress boiling off him in waves. "If you've done anything to jeopardize Melody's safety, you will pay. And I warn you. I do not make idle threats."

Fear flared in Clausen's eyes. Flushing beet purple, he took a step backward.

"Don't get your knickers in a wad, North. The crazy woman called in. Wanted to search a different sector. I couldn't stop her. She does her own thing."

True, and yet John didn't believe a word of the deputy's sputter. Something was wrong here. Something that could get Melody injured.

"Where was she going?" He collared Tad and shoved him toward the map. "Show me."

Sullenly, Tad poked at a spot off the grid, far out of the search range. "Here."

"Why would she go there?"

"I told you. She's crazy."

"If you're lying—" John stopped the rage building in his belly. "This isn't the first time you've withheld information from my department, is it, Clausen?"

The deputy remained sullen, arms crossed and eyes averted. John shoved the man's shoulder with his as he pushed past. He'd deal with Clausen later. Right now, Melody was out there alone on a bad ankle, not answering her radio.

That could only mean one thing.

She was in trouble.

CHAPTER FOURTEEN

SOMETHING WARM AND WET slashed across Melody's face. She tried to brush it away but her right arm wouldn't budge. The wet swipe came again. Struggling up from the darkness, Melody opened her eyes. The glaring sky overhead hurt her already banging head. Chili whined, slurped her face again and began to dig frantically at the hard snow with his front paws.

"Chili," she said, and her faithful friend leaned into her face, eyes worried.

Memory flooded back. The noise. The avalanche. A glance down revealed the problem. She was encased in concretelike snow up to her chest with only her head, shoulders and left arm free. Efforts to wiggle loose were useless. The problem with avalanche snow was that it hardened within seconds to form a rock-hard barrier nearly impossible to move without tools. The backpack beneath her held everything she needed but she couldn't move enough to reach it.

Her anxiety level, already at overload, jacked higher. She was in real trouble.

Unable to feel anything but bone-chilling cold from the waist down, she had to escape quickly before hypothermia took over.

Using her left hand, she began to dig and pound at the icy

covering over her other arm. With two arms free, she could make better progress. Without a shovel, her efforts produced little. Chili prowled restlessly, alternating between face licks and digging.

"Help me, Chili. Dig, boy, dig."

The well-trained animal had worked avalanche disasters before. At her command, he pawed with renewed energy. A cloud of snow flew out behind him.

She had no way of knowing how much time passed, but her one usable arm grew increasingly exhausted. Soon she was scooping tiny handfuls of snow at slower and slower speed. Her teeth rattled and her upper body shook so violently her back ached from the stress.

If only she could reach her shovel.

She attempted once more to shift positions. But she was stuck fast. And tired. So tired. She needed to rest. Just for a minute.

Chili licked her face and she snapped awake. Succumbing to the cold and fatigue was a mistake. To survive, she had to keep fighting.

More time passed. She had no idea how much, but the shivering stopped. She could no longer feel her left hand and let it fall to the snow, useless.

The sky's glare hurt too much. She closed her eyes. Chili licked her face again. She tried to look at him, but failed.

As the darkness crept in, Melody had one final thought. If only she had lived to apologize to John and to tell him she loved him.

John tramped along Connor Ridge, alternately yelling and whistling for Melody. Before leaving the command center, he'd sent out the call for more searchers. Those who had searched all morning for the child were too exhausted, so he'd called in reinforcements that would arrive within the next few hours. But for John, every minute that ticked past was another minute Melody—his Melody—was out there alone.

Unable to stand by and do nothing, he'd authorized Sheriff Page to handle the command post and he'd begun his own search. The Sheriff had clapped him on the back and with understanding in his eyes, said, "Go on, son. You're no good here until you find your lady."

His lady. Yes, she was his lady. And he should have told her so.

He'd snowmobiled as far into the search area as possible, but much of the terrain was accessible only on foot. Clausen had known that when he'd allowed Melody to come this way. Why hadn't he refused her request? The man had seen her ankle. He knew she couldn't hike these icy rocks and snow boulders.

The snowfall picked up as he traversed the ridge. Face numb from more than an hour of hiking, John could only think of one thing. If he was cold after an hour, what kind of shape was Melody in?

"Melody!" he called. Blowing snow filled his mouth.

As he hiked and called, John considered the worst. Melody had been gone too long without radio contact. She was either hurt or lost, and neither option was promising.

A thousand times over John wished he'd done things differently this morning. He should have told her how precious she was to him. He should have told her he loved her and would do everything in his power to help her work through her fear. He should have promised to earn her trust.

Angry at his stubborn pride, he jabbed a trekking pole hard into the snow and ice-covered ground. Jerking hard to dislodge it, he stumbled and began to slide. Adrenaline squirted through his veins. With a last-second surge of effort, he grabbed onto an outcrop of rock and stopped the slide. He had to get a grip, both physically and mentally. If he fell off the mountain, he was no good to Melody.

Whistle to his lips, he blew long and hard, then paused to listen. Off to his right, in the brush, he caught the faint rustling sound of movement. Most likely, he'd startled a deer, but he waited just the same, hope a living thing inside him.

Another sound came, louder now. The creature was advancing, not retreating. Breath held, John strained to hear. Was it his imagination or was that a dog's quick, sharp bark?

His heartbeat ratcheted up, so loud he couldn't hear anything else.

Suddenly, a red, snow-laced dog in an orange SAR vest burst into sight on a slight rise above him. Alone.

Dear God, where was Melody?

"Chili! Come here, boy. Come here."

John started to run toward the animal, cursing the thick snow and slick rocks for slowing him down. He panted, his frigid breaths making his lungs ache. He didn't care. Nothing mattered but finding Melody.

The dog moved faster and easier. In minutes, Chili jumped and leaped around John's legs, barking frantically.

John scanned the ridge and all around as far as he could see. Melody was nowhere in sight.

He'd heard her give the search command many times and prayed he did it properly. The dog knew where she was. Chili was his best hope of finding Melody.

"Where is she, Chili? Find Melody. Find your mama."

The dog spun around and headed back the way he'd

come. John followed as fast as his legs could, but many times the dog stopped, turning to bark as if urging the slow human to hurry.

They had crested a narrow ridge and started down the other side when Chili bolted ahead. Snow spun out around him, reminding John of the first time he'd seen Melody frolicking with her dogs. The memory of her beautiful laugh and the hope that he could make things right drove him to run, though his legs and lungs screamed to rest.

Chili's wild barking came again and the animal stopped, this time beside a mound of snow surrounded on two sides by jutting green spruce. Something blue and yellow protruded from the snowbank.

Once more, the gift of adrenaline kicked in. In seconds, John collapsed, panting, onto his knees beside Melody's cold, still form. Her skin was like wax, the bluish tinge frightening evidence of how long she'd been trapped in the snowslide. Her eyes were closed, the lashes crusted in snow.

A groan of despair rose in John's aching chest. Was he too late?

He felt the soft area of her throat, found a pulse faint and erratic but discernible, and nearly collapsed with relief. After a quick call for help, he yanked his shovel free from his backpack and began to dig. The valiant red dog added his efforts.

John refused to acknowledge the pain in his shoulders or the ache in his back. Over and over he chanted, "Stay with me, Mel. I love you. Stay with me."

When at last, the pile of snow relented, John pulled her free, stumbling and staggering back with the effort. He fell to his knees and drew her close to his work-heated body, wrapping her in the blankets from both their packs.

"Where is that chopper?" he barked into his radio and received assurances that help was in the air.

He unzipped his coat to bring Melody closer to his body heat. She was so terribly, frightfully cold. The search dog was clearly stressed, so John urged him onto his lap, as well. They were a sandwich, with Melody in between.

He touched her face with his gloved hand. "Melody."

She didn't stir.

Dropping his forehead to hers, he whispered all the things he'd wanted to say last night and hadn't. He could only hope she heard and understood.

He pressed his lips to hers and shuddered with dread at how cold and unresponsive they were. The back of his throat burned with the very real fear that he would lose her. He kissed her again and again, breathing warmth into her mouth, pleading with her to live.

He'd never been a praying man but there on that mountain, with his love in his arms, John North prayed for one more chance to make things right.

After what seemed an eternity, the whomp-whomp of the helicopter broke through the frozen silence. John tenderly kissed Melody's cold, still lips one last time and hoped that help had not come too late.

Melody awoke to warmth and snowy whiteness. The world smelled sterile and empty, but no longer cold.

Her stomach pitched. Was she still trapped in the snow-bank and suffering from the delusion of warmth? Wasn't that what happened right before death? Where was Chili? He would be distraught without her. If she was dead who would take him home?

"Oh, Chili, I'm sorry." She wasn't sure if she'd spoken aloud or if she'd only thought the apology.

"Miss Crawford?" A woman's bespectacled face peered over a set of metal rails. She wore a plastic name tag and a white uniform.

Melody blinked, trying to clear the cobwebs. A nurse? Was she in a hospital?

She had the courage then to glance around at her environment. No snowbank. No dark, jutting spruce. No granite mountain faces. Instead, a TV hung from the wall. Next to it, some kind of machine beeped and flashed numbers. A small nightstand was to her left. An ugly green, vinyl chair sat in one corner.

Relief trickled through her as warm and welcome as the heated blankets surrounding her tired, achy body. Someone had found her. She was safe.

She tried to speak, but only a rusty croak came out. Her tongue felt thick and heavy and her throat raw.

The nurse smiled. "Try this."

She held a cup to Melody's mouth and supported her head while she drank. A salty, wonderfully warm liquid slipped over her tongue and down her throat.

"Better?"

Melody nodded and lay back, shaky from the effort. She blew out a sigh. "Thank you." Though slurred, the words were heartfelt. "Where's my dog?"

The nurse's look was quizzical. "I'm sorry. I don't know anything about a dog."

Someone needed to take care of her dogs. There was only person she would trust with her animals. John.

The ugly memory rushed in as if it had been waiting to

attack. Somehow she must swallow her pride and beg John to look after her dogs—after she told him the truth.

Fully alert now, Melody became aware of the tingling pain in her right hand. She tried to flex her fingers and found them stiff and puffy. Leaning up to examine them, she discovered IV fluids dripping into her arm.

"Are you hurting?" The nurse hovered nearby, checking monitors and watching her.

"I'm fine."

"I was warned you'd say that."

Warned? She turned her head to stare at the nurse. "By whom?"

"The tall, good-looking man outside the door wearing holes in the tile. The man who saved your life. Why don't I tell him you're awake?"

John was here?

"John saved my life? How?"

The nurse glanced up from adjusting the IV pump. "You don't remember?"

"All I remember is being tired and cold and trying desperately to dig myself out of an avalanche. And then nothing."

"The helicopter brought you in. Apparently, your hero wouldn't stop searching until he found you. You must have been up there awhile. The paramedics said your man was a basket case, barking orders, demanding that they be careful with you, keep you warm and get you off that mountain at record speed."

"I don't understand. John found me?"

How had he known where to look? How had he known she was in trouble?

The nurse nodded. "Pretty special guy you have, I think.

He was hypothermic himself, but insisted you receive the medical attention and the chopper ride. He hiked out of there on his own. All the nurses are calling him a hero. You're a lucky woman."

Melody rested back against the stiff pillow, taking in the information. John had come for her, even though he'd had no way of knowing where she was or that she'd been caught in an avalanche. He'd come looking, and he had not given up until he'd found her.

At that moment, the door swished open and the man himself stormed inside, face set in a determined scowl. "I heard voices. Is she awake?"

The nurse arched an amused eyebrow at Melody. "Is he always this impatient?"

Melody thought of exactly how patient John North could be and blushed, shaking her head. "Not always."

Halfway to the bedside, John stopped, hovering there until the nurse departed, hands shoved into his coat pockets. He looked uncharacteristically uncertain and Melody's chest swelled with love. Even if he didn't want to hear it, she'd been given a second chance. He would not leave this room without knowing her feelings for him.

"Where's Chili?" she asked.

"At home. He's doing great. Just worried about you. Like the rest of us."

"Did you really save my life?"

"Somebody had to. Stubborn woman, going off by yourself on a bad ankle. I won't let you do that again. No partner, no search. End of subject." He paced from one end of the room to the other and back again. "You could have died, you know. You almost did."

"John."

He didn't answer. He was on a roll now, with a full head of steam. For the next couple of minutes, she let him bluster and rave. And with every word, her hopes grew brighter.

The big tough Ranger chewed her up one side and down the other. He complained about her independence and then he praised it. He threatened to blacklist her from volunteering and then he told her how good she and Chili were at their jobs.

Melody lifted a hand, let it fall onto the snowy sheet and tried again. "John. Please."

In midpace, he did an about-face that would have made his superiors proud.

"What?" It was more a bark than a word.

"I'm sorry." Sorry he'd had to rescue her. Sorry for last night.

All the bluster went out of the big man. He opened his mouth to say more and then clapped it shut again. He slammed both fists onto his hips, dropped his head and released a loud, gusty sigh.

"Are you all right? Really? Do you hurt anywhere?" He shoved splayed fingers through his hair. "Do you need pain medicine? I can get the nurse back in here in two seconds flat."

She bet he could, too, but the nurse had no medication for the pain in Melody's heart.

"I'm fine."

He huffed. "Save it for someone who believes you."

"My fingers and toes are tingly." Painfully so. "That's all."

"No surprise there. You suffered some early frostbite, but the doctors say you'll recover to do something else dangerous." He said the last as if he would tear into her again.

She reached for his hand, pulling it against her heart. "I was scared, John. I prayed you'd come."

John closed his eyes as if the admission was too painful to bear. When he looked at her again, the ravages of worry and fear and fatigue were there in his dark eyes for her to witness.

"What if I hadn't? Dear God, what if I hadn't found you?" he asked, warm, calloused fingers caressing her cheek. "I was scared too, sweetheart, more scared than I've ever been. When I found you there beneath all that snow, I thought—"

"You thought what?"

Sincere brown eyes swept her face. His jaw flexed. His Adam's apple rose and fell. When he spoke, the words were a husky whisper.

"You were so cold. So terribly cold. I thought I'd lost you for good."

His voice choked. He gulped back the emotion, but Melody saw what he couldn't say. The gaping hole in her heart was suddenly filled. John wasn't angry. He was afraid of losing her.

The realization hit her hard and fast. All these weeks she'd pushed him away because of his military background. And yet, even after she'd hurt him last night and driven him away, he'd traipsed through the bitter cold with unrelenting determination to find her and keep her safe.

He'd said she could trust him. And she knew it was true. It always had been.

"John North," she whispered, touching his beloved, whisker-roughened jaw. "I love you."

"What did you say?" His voice was incredulous.

"I love you." Anxiety made her fingers tremble, but she was determined to carry on. She'd sworn if she survived, another day would not pass without telling him.

When he only stared, she hurried to say, "It's okay if you don't feel the same."

It wasn't at all okay, but she was determined he should know. "Nearly dying makes a person realize many things. I kept thinking of the ugly way we'd parted and that you would never know how grateful I am to you and how you've made me a better person. But most of all, you've brought love back into my life. You're my hero in every sense of the word. And I love you, whether you love me or not. I love you."

John squeezed his eyes closed and shuddered once, hard. And then he did the sweetest thing. He went to one knee beside her bed, big hands sandwiching hers.

"Melody Crawford, I've loved you since the first time I heard you laugh."

Joy sprang up behind her rib cage and spread to her mouth. "You have?"

"Yes ma'am. Last night I tried and failed to show you."

Melody shook her head, denying him. "You didn't fail. I felt your love, but I was afraid of it, afraid of being vulnerable."

"Are you afraid now?"

"Only of losing you."

"Ah, sweetheart. That is not going to happen. Say you'll marry me."

Laughter bubbled up and tears of happiness dampened her eyelashes. "I'll marry you."

John rose and gathered her into his arms. "And have my babies?"

The sweet question released a helium balloon of joy inside her. "Oh, yes. Babies. Your babies. All the babies you want."

Melody lifted her face for his kiss. In his warm brown eyes she saw the promise of the future, a future she thought had died seventeen years ago with a gunshot to the head and with the resulting bitterness and fear.

Now, the joy of being able to feel again, to love again, to be the wife of John North, was all she'd ever ask of life.

EPILOGUE

THEY WERE MARRIED in late June when the blue columbine fragranced the green, grassy meadow and the warblers sang a merry mating song above Glass Falls. The majestic mountains rose around the setting, high and purple and kissed with snow. And from them flowed the rush and roar of pristine waters, splashing down into the white foaming creek. Here, in the outdoors was the perfect place for a wedding, at least to John and Melody.

A handful of people, friends and family, had gathered to add their blessing to the union. Heart full, John gazed around at the small gathering while waiting for the moment he could finally claim Melody forever.

His mother and dad were all smiles with the grandkids dancing around their legs. He smiled, too, to think of giving them more babies to love.

All the former thoughts that he was not made for marriage had been nothing but pride. He hated to fail and he'd failed once.

Melody squeezed his arm and pointed to an eagle lazily soaring overhead. He looked at the noble bird, but then turned his gaze back to Melody. He could look at his beautiful bride forever. And he knew without a shadow of a doubt, with Melody by his side, he would not fail.

Sheriff Brent Page and his wife came up, good people, John thought. Though very different in style and age, Emma Page and Melody had become friends.

"Ready for the ball and chain, North?" the sheriff kidded and received a whack on the arm and an indulgent laugh from his wife.

"Can't wait," he answered truthfully.

Page patted his wife's hand. "Nothing helps a man like a good woman. And I think you found one."

"Yes, sir, I did." His gaze automatically sought out Melody. She was crouched down talking to his nephew.

"Before the shindig kicks off I thought you'd want to know the D.A. is pursuing charges against Clausen."

"Good."

Tad Clausen had been fired when his intentional sabotage of the Emergency Management Department was discovered. The disgraced former deputy immediately packed his family and moved to Denver. But his actions had been more than vicious jealousy; they'd been criminal. John was glad to know the D.A. agreed.

He still shuddered to think of how close he'd come to losing Melody when the deputy sent her on that wild goose chase outside her assigned sector. If he'd had his way, he would have throttled the man himself. Now he could rest easy knowing the courts would take care of Tad Clausen.

"I hope he's learned his lesson. Sorry to cost you a deputy."

"Better no deputy than a conniving one who doesn't care about the people he serves."

John had to concur. He was about to say as much when his bride started toward him and he lost all thought.

"Ready?" she asked, her words a bit breathy.

"Yes, ma'am. I was ready a long time ago." He kissed her on the nose. "You look gorgeous."

She'd insisted on simplicity, but even in the short white dress with a simple wreath of blue columbine circling her head, Melody's black hair and stunning eyes stood out.

"So do you," she said.

He smiled into those eyes and thought how deep and precious was the love and trust he saw there. And he planned to spend the rest of his life treasuring both.

Holding hands, they walked to the designated area where the attendants waited. The minister, a hearty young man who skied and climbed on a regular basis, opened his Bible and began to read.

Melody listened to the ancient words in awe and amazement. She'd never dared dream of finding a man like John North. A man she could trust with her life as well as with her heart.

And yet, here she stood, more sure of him than of anything in her entire life. Somehow, with his insistent love, he'd erased her fears and opened her eyes to all the beautiful things she'd been missing. He'd even convinced her to give talks to schoolkids, instinctively knowing she'd love it. He'd been right.

Her beloved had been right about so many things. And she would ever be thankful that he'd stubbornly pushed his way into her life, loving her until she'd come to her senses.

In her heart Melody knew she had changed for the better. She would always be a strong, independent woman, but with John by her side, she would be more than that. She would be free from the bonds of despair and free to be the loving woman who had been hiding for so many years.

Her lips quavered as she spoke the beautiful promises, but

she quavered, not with anxiety, but with emotion too strong to repress.

John's hand shook in hers as he promised to love and care for her for all times. Melody's throat filled with the beauty. Her big, tough, confident man trembled with love for her.

As the last vow quivered on the wind, the minister asked, "Are there rings?"

Melody and John smiled into each other's eyes and then turned to their two attendants. Chili and Ace, handsomely dressed in black-and-white vests, sat patiently at their heels. Each carried a gold band on a ribbon around his neck.

The onlookers chuckled as Melody and John removed the rings, quieting when the minister received them for a blessing. Holding the golden circles high, he spoke of their symbolic nature. He talked of the gold as a cherished treasure whose value never faded, just as the love of a man and woman was an unfading treasure to cherish. And then he spoke of the circular shape which had no beginning and no end, signifying eternal love.

And as Melody slipped the gold band onto John's strong, wide hand and then stepped into her groom's embrace, the circle of love she'd longed for all these lonely years was finally and forever complete.

MILLS & BOON®
Pure reading pleasure™

NOVEMBER 2008 HARDBACK TITLES

ROMANCE

The Billionaire's Bride of Vengeance *Miranda Lee*	978 0 263 20382 0
The Santangeli Marriage *Sara Craven*	978 0 263 20383 7
The Spaniard's Virgin Housekeeper *Diana Hamilton*	978 0 263 20384 4
The Greek Tycoon's Reluctant Bride *Kate Hewitt*	978 0 263 20385 1
Innocent Mistress, Royal Wife *Robyn Donald*	978 0 263 20386 8
Taken for Revenge, Bedded for Pleasure *India Grey*	978 0 263 20387 5
The Billionaire Boss's Innocent Bride *Lindsay Armstrong*	978 0 263 20388 2
The Billionaire's Defiant Wife *Amanda Browning*	978 0 263 20389 9
Nanny to the Billionaire's Son *Barbara McMahon*	978 0 263 20390 5
Cinderella and the Sheikh *Natasha Oakley*	978 0 263 20391 2
Promoted: Secretary to Bride! *Jennie Adams*	978 0 263 20392 9
The Black Sheep's Proposal *Patricia Thayer*	978 0 263 20393 6
The Snow-Kissed Bride *Linda Goodnight*	978 0 263 20394 3
The Rancher's Runaway Princess *Donna Alward*	978 0 263 20395 0
The Greek Doctor's New-Year Baby *Kate Hardy*	978 0 263 20396 7
The Wife He's Been Waiting For *Dianne Drake*	978 0 263 20397 4

HISTORICAL

The Captain's Forbidden Miss *Margaret McPhee*	978 0 263 20216 8
The Earl and the Hoyden *Mary Nichols*	978 0 263 20217 5
From Governess to Society Bride *Helen Dickson*	978 0 263 20218 2

MEDICAL™

The Heart Surgeon's Secret Child *Meredith Webber*	978 0 263 19918 5
The Midwife's Little Miracle *Fiona McArthur*	978 0 263 19919 2
The Single Dad's New-Year Bride *Amy Andrews*	978 0 263 19920 8
Posh Doc Claims His Bride *Anne Fraser*	978 0 263 19921 5

MILLS & BOON®
Pure reading pleasure™

NOVEMBER 2008 LARGE PRINT TITLES

ROMANCE

Bought for Revenge, Bedded for Pleasure *Emma Darcy*	978 0 263 20090 4
Forbidden: The Billionaire's Virgin Princess *Lucy Monroe*	978 0 263 20091 1
The Greek Tycoon's Convenient Wife *Sharon Kendrick*	978 0 263 20092 8
The Marciano Love-Child *Melanie Milburne*	978 0 263 20093 5
Parents in Training *Barbara McMahon*	978 0 263 20094 2
Newlyweds of Convenience *Jessica Hart*	978 0 263 20095 9
The Desert Prince's Proposal *Nicola Marsh*	978 0 263 20096 6
Adopted: Outback Baby *Barbara Hannay*	978 0 263 20097 3

HISTORICAL

The Virtuous Courtesan *Mary Brendan*	978 0 263 20172 7
The Homeless Heiress *Anne Herries*	978 0 263 20173 4
Rebel Lady, Convenient Wife *June Francis*	978 0 263 20174 1

MEDICAL™

Nurse Bride, Bayside Wedding *Gill Sanderson*	978 0 263 19986 4
Billionaire Doctor, Ordinary Nurse *Carol Marinelli*	978 0 263 19987 1
The Sheikh Surgeon's Baby *Meredith Webber*	978 0 263 19988 8
The Outback Doctor's Surprise Bride *Amy Andrews*	978 0 263 19989 5
A Wedding at Limestone Coast *Lucy Clark*	978 0 263 19990 1
The Doctor's Meant-To-Be Marriage *Janice Lynn*	978 0 263 19991 8

MILLS & BOON

Pure reading pleasure™

DECEMBER 2008 HARDBACK TITLES

ROMANCE

The Ruthless Magnate's Virgin Mistress *Lynne Graham*	978 0 263 20398 1
The Greek's Forced Bride *Michelle Reid*	978 0 263 20399 8
The Sheikh's Rebellious Mistress *Sandra Marton*	978 0 263 20400 1
The Prince's Waitress Wife *Sarah Morgan*	978 0 263 20401 8
Bought for the Sicilian Billionaire's Bed *Sharon Kendrick*	978 0 263 20402 5
Count Maxime's Virgin *Susan Stephens*	978 0 263 20403 2
The Italian's Ruthless Baby Bargain *Margaret Mayo*	978 0 263 20404 9
Valenti's One-Month Mistress *Sabrina Philips*	978 0 263 20405 6
The Australian's Society Bride *Margaret Way*	978 0 263 20406 3
The Royal Marriage Arrangement *Rebecca Winters*	978 0 263 20407 0
Two Little Miracles *Caroline Anderson*	978 0 263 20408 7
Manhattan Boss, Diamond Proposal *Trish Wylie*	978 0 263 20409 4
Her Valentine Blind Date *Raye Morgan*	978 0 263 20410 0
The Bridesmaid and the Billionaire *Shirley Jump*	978 0 263 20411 7
Children's Doctor, Society Bride *Joanna Neil*	978 0 263 20412 4
Outback Doctor, English Bride *Leah Martyn*	978 0 263 20413 1

HISTORICAL

Marrying the Mistress *Juliet Landon*	978 0 263 20219 9
To Deceive a Duke *Amanda McCabe*	978 0 263 20220 5
Knight of Grace *Sophia James*	978 0 263 20221 2

MEDICAL™

The Heart Surgeon's Baby Surprise *Meredith Webber*	978 0 263 19922 2
A Wife for the Baby Doctor *Josie Metcalfe*	978 0 263 19923 9
The Royal Doctor's Bride *Jessica Matthews*	978 0 263 19924 6
Surgeon Boss, Surprise Dad *Janice Lynn*	978 0 263 19925 3

MILLS & BOON®
Pure reading pleasure™

DECEMBER 2008 LARGE PRINT TITLES

ROMANCE

Hired: The Sheikh's Secretary Mistress *Lucy Monroe*	978 0 263 20098 0
The Billionaire's Blackmailed Bride *Jacqueline Baird*	978 0 263 20099 7
The Sicilian's Innocent Mistress *Carole Mortimer*	978 0 263 20100 0
The Sheikh's Defiant Bride *Sandra Marton*	978 0 263 20101 7
Wanted: Royal Wife and Mother *Marion Lennox*	978 0 263 20102 4
The Boss's Unconventional Assistant *Jennie Adams*	978 0 263 20103 1
Inherited: Instant Family *Judy Christenberry*	978 0 263 20104 8
The Prince's Secret Bride *Raye Morgan*	978 0 263 20105 5

HISTORICAL

Miss Winthorpe's Elopement *Christine Merrill*	978 0 263 20175 8
The Rake's Unconventional Mistress *Juliet Landon*	978 0 263 20176 5
Rags-to-Riches Bride *Mary Nichols*	978 0 263 20177 2

MEDICAL™

Single Dad Seeks a Wife *Melanie Milburne*	978 0 263 19992 5
Her Four-Year Baby Secret *Alison Roberts*	978 0 263 19993 2
Country Doctor, Spring Bride *Abigail Gordon*	978 0 263 19994 9
Marrying the Runaway Bride *Jennifer Taylor*	978 0 263 19995 6
The Midwife's Baby *Fiona McArthur*	978 0 263 19996 3
The Fatherhood Miracle *Margaret Barker*	978 0 263 19997 0